BEAUTIFUL DECEPTION

A Dark Mafia Romance

Agostino Crime Family Series Book III

DAHLIA REIGN

About This Book

I was taken from the comfort of my own home and subjected to hell. Even after I escaped, I was never free… Not from my captor, and not from the voices he left inside my head.

I was hunting for answers that pointed to a grave, though the question hung in the air: who was at the bottom of those six feet?

I'm Persephone. And this is my story of filthy sex, dangerous revenge, and broken hearts. Don't cry for me; they didn't. No, cry for those who cross my path.

Dedication

*This is for the thousands who suffer from mental illness and do so in silence.
You're not alone. There are so many more just like you, some in the light and
others shrouded in darkness. Ask for help. Don't suffer alone.
Because, together, we are powerful.*

Prologue
PERSEPHONE-PAST

Seconds turned to minutes. Minutes into hours. Hours into days. The never-ending whimpers and pleas from those who surrounded me were grating on my limited sanity. I needed peace. I wanted to yell and rage—tug my hair out as I got in their faces—to tell them that no one cared about them now.

Us. No one cared about *us*.

Our stories may have all begun differently, but they would all align in the middle. And—even more sadly—the end. Our ending wouldn't be a happily ever after. We were all well and truly fucked at this point; there would be no surviving this existence. And it would be no more than an *existence* because wherever this took us, it wouldn't be a life. It would be hell on earth.

The room smelled of mold, urine, and desperation—a heady combination that made me want to choke on my own vomit. My wrists were sore from the tight rope cutting off my circulation. And my limbs and brain felt sluggish, a side effect of whatever concoction they gave me to keep me quiet.

They didn't like the fire in me, so they tried to extinguish it with the underside of their boots. I was pretty sure my ribs were broken, my right eye was swollen shut, and blood had been trickling down my face from my hairline. Pain was an incredible thing. For some people, it made them weak. Pliable. Not me. I came alive. And I could assure you I'd known serious fucking pain in my life.

Every single kick or punch, every grunt and slur thrown at me, and every single assault they presented was stored accordingly. To me, time slowed down and I became attuned to every minute detail when I focused through the agony. I added them to my vault, the one that held all my secrets. The same mausoleum, that one day, I would unlock to unleash holy terror on every single person residing inside.

I'd do everything in my power to ensure I got the hell out of here and made all of them pay. It was a silent promise I would offer every single whimpering girl in this room. They didn't deserve this; no one did. I'd avenge them.

"Look who's finally awake," black hood number one said from above me.

You could tell by the way he walked and talked he may very well be the boss. His eyes were an interesting shade of brown—neither dark nor light—just literal brown. There was a fervor beneath them, one that would suggest if I touched his dick, he'd probably be hard.

My heart was pounding as a gloved hand smeared my own blood across my face. Ever so slowly, the sick bastard put his finger in his mouth and moaned. The fucker… *moaned*.

"You're pretty fucked in the head, aren't you?" I asked, grunting as I twisted the bindings around my wrists. "Mama didn't love you enough? Or was it too much?"

He stared like he was picking at my brain, attempting to learn all my secrets, as if his glare could scan every detail. His arms and face were concealed, nothing overly discernable about him besides those eyes.

"Such a tough girl," he whispered.

I'd met my match. There was no way to distinguish him from anyone else in the crowd, because the controlled volume meant he wasn't using his vocal cords. There was some sound but not enough vibration in order to detect those particular markers I used to file away the precise acoustics.

"I know your secret, little one." He continued his charade as he bent closer to my ear. "That mind of yours is working quickly. What have you catalogued so far?"

Motherfucker.

"Fuck you." My defenses dropped rapidly, morphing into anger.

"Don't let me down, Persephone. I know you're scouring for details. Tell me, have you found any?" Those brown eyes read me like a book.

Not many people knew what I was capable of, or how I focused on things. They just didn't understand the speed in which my mind worked—the way I was forced to take in everything around me. Yet, *he* did. His gaze was guarded but amused; he wanted me to confess my sins.

When I didn't answer, he shook his head. "Such a disappointment." He rose to his feet, his displeasure the only thing he left unmasked.

"Pl-please. No!" One of the girls cried out as a man grabbed her by the arm, twisting it to force her to move. Even from where I lay on the ground, I could tell her captor was bothered by her reaction and the pain he'd caused her.

Their ringleader ordered him to bring the girl over. The three of them had a conversation too far away to hear anything above the girl's whimpering. Well, I couldn't hear the exchange, but it appeared as though *she* could. And I guessed it was really, really fucking bad.

The brown-eyed man leaned down to the girl's ear, and I watched wetness appear at the apex of her thighs before soaking her denim shorts. Then, ever so slowly, it trickled down her bare legs and onto the floor. The fucker holding her looked as if he wanted to be sick; conflict blazed in his eyes as the girl was removed from his grasp.

They stood there for a few more moments as the guy evidently in charge talked and pointed around the room. The other man nodded a few times, and I could see the indecision on his face dissipate, little by little. They both turned to stare at my prone figure, my agony humming in perfect harmony with their perusal, before dropping to their haunches beside me.

"Without sacrifice, there is no great reward," Brown Eyes whispered to the man next to him. "The elite use the weak to make those sacrifices and take the reward."

Christ. What a fucking masochist.

"Yes, sir." The muscular goon conceded, his face devoid of the remorse he'd shown moments ago. "Want me to take care of her?"

"Yes." Blankness stared back at me before the hooded figure nodded. "She's just like the rest." I flinched at his words—the sudden abrasive meaning hitting me hard, for a reason I couldn't explain.

The man leaned down and grabbed my arm, tugging me to my knees. Pain roared through my body. I rose to my feet—my movements fumbling and awkward—before leaning against him as he unlocked my wrists from the latch on the wall. My entire body was sluggish. Weak.

"You feel real tough, don't you? Dragging a drugged and beaten woman around, taking orders from a man with a dick bigger than yours," I said in a voice that was stronger than I felt—because, well, *fuck him.*

"We'll see how tough you are when your ass is being pounded by three dudes at once, all to break you in for your new owner." He chuckled but it wasn't sincere.

"Pussy." I spit in his face, enjoying the flare of disgust I'd finally elicited.

"Hey!" Another one of the idiots yelled in the background, garnering my handler's attention. "Boss wants that one."

My hands had long since lost sensation, and my legs shook as they moved on autopilot, forcing me out of the urine-saturated metal crate. We approached an SUV, and I was thrown into the back seat with the man in question. I'd been right. Brown Eyes was the captain steering this sick ship.

He was over six feet, with a somewhat masculine body, definitely not an avid gym-goer but still strong. He was texting on his phone and ignoring me as I struggled to get comfortable. My hands were a nasty shade of purple from the tightened rope, and I couldn't feel a damn thing.

His suit was three pieces and expensive—several thousands of dollars. He filled it out nicely, but it was a strange contrast to the dumb ski mask on his face. Some of his men wore them. And others didn't—the expendables. Even his shoes were shiny, untarnished, and screamed money. Apparently, the skin trade was lucrative.

"Tell me, Persephone, what have you learned here?" His eyes were dark and challenging—much like earlier.

"How about you take that stupid hood off and talk to me." I smirked, twitching in my seat.

"Don't play dumb. You're cataloging everything in here." He tapped my forehead with his leather glove. "Spill." His voice control was pissing me off.

He was intelligent. Cunning. That much was true. And doing his research on each person he took. It was a smart way to do business. I'm sure none of the women in that container were from families with any clout. They'd be reported missing, but never heard from again.

"I don't know what you mean." I decided to play dumb. "I just want you to fucking drop dead." I gave him a saccharine smile.

"Don't be coy. We both know your secret." He grabbed my bindings and tugged me closer. "I've read all about you, Persephone. Prone to violent outbursts. A long record of assault and vigilante behavior. And your IQ is off the charts."

"Fuck you." I licked my lips, his eyes following the motion. "What do you want?"

I was losing my grip on my limited sanity. I hated not being in control, and his constant scrutiny was wearing on my nerves. My heart rate was increasing, and I started sweating as my mind sought safety in the dark caverns of my brain. Once I stepped on that path, I wouldn't escape until I caused major damage—to myself and those around me. I was a ticking time bomb.

I'd been subjected to years of therapy, and I still had no coping mechanism to calm me past a certain point. I'd get lost in my head, then shipped off to a psychiatric ward until I was released.

Sociopathic tendencies. Lack of empathy. Mental inhibitions caused by a high IQ and lack of social cues. There was no remedy they could find. I just needed someone who could cage my beast. But I wouldn't hold my breath with the misguided assumption that, that person actually existed.

"You." His expression was blank as he finally answered my question. "I've amassed an empire by surrounding myself with skilled individuals. I want you… at my side, as I rule."

"Me?" I didn't know if I wanted to laugh or lash out. The extra tug on my ropes told me he knew I was struggling to maintain control.

Suddenly, the car swerved, and my body was thrown against his hard chest; he released me and shoved me to the floor. He pulled out his gun and his phone from under his jacket, simultaneously. He was giving orders in Italian, but his voice… he maintained his anonymity.

He dropped his phone and rolled down his window, just as the rear of the car was riddled with bullets. Fucking Christ. Why couldn't I catch a damn break? The metal projectiles erupted against the vehicle, and my captor's gun was rapidly firing as melee continued around us. A moan came from the driver. Forcing myself onto my knees, I leaned over his seat.

"He's fucking dead!" Before either of us could act, the car plowed through a concrete barrier and jackknifed into the air.

My body lifted with the motion, slamming forward as the SUV landed in the Hudson River. The windshield smashed open, and we bobbed for a few moments, both of us rattled from the impact. Then realization settled in and terror flooded my system. I couldn't swim and the damn car was filling with water.

"Fuck." He growled over the sound of our demise rushing in around us.

The dark-brown liquid had risen to my waist, and my body was losing its battle with exhaustion. My bound hands were unable to wedge the door open, and I knew I'd be forced to die next to this asshole.

"Hold the fuck still." I barely registered the knife he used to cut through the rope. "Let's go."

He grabbed my hand, pulling me through the shattered windshield and pushing me towards the surface. My lungs were seizing with a desperate need for air as I tried to move my arms. I could feel the darkness beckoning me home—the peaceful divide that became my solace when life was too much. Suddenly, my chest filled with air, and my captor shouted orders around me just as the sweet oblivion took hold and I was lost to the obscurity of my own mind.

I woke with a start, lying on sheets that were worn and scratchy against my skin and reeked of urine and the metallic scent of blood. Steel bars boxed me in, and I had no doubt I was in a basement. My mouth was dry, my head was pounding, and I was so hungry. I sat up slowly, trying to get my bearings as movement in the corner caught my attention.

"Sorry, sweetness." Brown eyes stood several feet away, looming in the darkness. His mask was removed but the shadows hid his facial details. His voice was louder, but my mind was too foggy to register it.

"What?" I held my head in my hands.

"You're a liability I can't have right now," he said, his tone calm and unaffected. "Can't have you gunning for me after seeing my face."

"I haven't." I was being sincere. "And I can't focus on your voice yet."

His silence told me he didn't believe me, but it was true.

"Pity." He turned his back on me and headed towards a metal door. A wide man with a gigantic nose and dirty jeans stepped into the room, nodding in respect as he past. "We could've had fun. You could've been useful to me."

"I'll find you, then I'll… Fucking. Ruin. You." I growled at his retreating form.

"Of that, I have no doubt. But you'll have to catch me first." And then he was gone, the metal door slamming behind him.

"Are you hungry?" the dirty man asked, unlocking the cage and forcing me to crawl out.

I dropped to my stomach as pain roared across my back—over and over again. I tried to roll onto my side, but his heavy boot stepped between my shoulder blades and held me against the cold ground. I could see his shadow move as he raised his arm, then brought it down fast and hard against my spine. I couldn't hold back the scream that erupted. Pain, I could normally handle, but now all I could do was think about how fucking much this hurt. A whip. I held onto its sound, ignoring the sting and losing count of his strikes

"Mr. Yamada won't tolerate disobedience. You will eat when he tells you to." *Smack.* "You will beg when he tells you to. You will take a piss, only when he tells you to." *Smack. Smack.*

He continued his tirade with each sentence. Japanese. I was being sold to the Japanese. This wasn't the first time a man had tried to rule my life, and I was sure it wouldn't be the last. As in, I was getting the fuck out of here. I refused to live out my days eating rice hand fed to me by a master barking commands I wouldn't understand.

Thirty-four days. It took me thirty-four days of training to be shipped off to Mr. Yamada. Thirteen people. I killed thirteen people to escape certain peril and punishment.

I would learn the toughest lesson of all while I enacted my revenge: not everything was as it seems. An author could tell you a simple story, but each reader would have their own perception in the end. This was my story of revenge. A harrowing plot of rage and torment, mixed with savage sex with a delicious fucking monster. But wait until the end before you judge the choices I made. Because New York would see me again and when it did... no one was safe.

I was going to release my demons and hunt down every last bastard who'd hurt me. And good old Brown Eyes was at the top of my list. I wouldn't just stick to henchmen... I'd destroy their entire ring. Rats lived in colonies—you needed to kill their king so the rest starved.

The heavy base pounding through the speakers made the office door vibrate. My boss, Carmine Ragetti, sat with his younger brother, Matteo, staring at me like they were bored. I'd been sniffing out details, thanks to Carmine's crew, and it was about time I left California and headed back to New York.

His family ruled the west coast, a formidable force of brothers with a vendetta against the New York mafia. Carmine hired me when I first hit the Golden State, put me under his protection. As I got closer to them, I learned we had a lot more in common than any of us expected.

Carmine was the eldest son of John Michael Ragetti, head of the west coast faction of the mafia. His Uncle Sal was arranged to marry a woman by the name of Serafina. When the man came to New York to collect his bride, he was murdered. The very next day,

Serafina was betrothed to none other than Anthony Moretti—the heir of a rival mafia family in New York.

Carmine's crew helped me scour the dark net and were able to track a shipping container that was transported to some docks on the east coast, owned by the Agostino Family. The Agostinos ran New York—and the Morettis—so we were curious as to what this all meant.

"Pretty face, nice tits, and a brain. Who would've known?" Carmine stared at me as I raised my chin higher. It didn't matter that I was dressed in only a G-string and clear heels; my nose remained in the air.

"Talk shit and I leave without helping you," I growled, baiting him into an argument. But he knew if he engaged, the information he wanted would come with an additional cost.

"You fuckin' the computer geek for information?" His tone deepened, and I knew he was begging for a fight. Carmine liked to pretend he loved submission, but he really lived for a little bit of spirit.

Most women took one look at his over-six-foot height, his wide, muscular frame—every inch covered in tattoos—and they'd run away screaming. He found solace in bending his conquests to his will, but his true fire burned bright when a woman didn't cower. I felt bad for whoever would one day make him fall to his knees.

"Just cause I'm a stripper doesn't mean I fuck everyone." I folded my arms across my chest, pushing my breasts higher as his eyes followed the motion.

"So, it was sent to the Agostino port… and what? They own it and people pay them to use it. Doesn't mean the container was delivered to them," he countered, his patience dwindling.

"Duh." He growled at my disrespect. "It was sent to a dummy corp we tracked—the one tied to the Morettis," I explained further.

His scowl morphed into a smile at the mention of his long-time adversaries. His need for vengeance against that family filled the air. But he wouldn't make a move just yet, not with his father still in control. And definitely not without a plan and a bargaining chip.

"You going to New York?" I nodded in response to his question. "Matteo will go with you."

"No. Give me time to see what I can do. I've got an audition at *Spogliato*." My words tightened his jaw.

"Perse, this isn't some small organization. Those two families are constantly at each other's throats, and you don't need to be in the center of it. Especially not with us on the other side of the country."

"Careful, Carmine. I wouldn't want word to get out that you're a pussy… for pussy." I cackled, smirking as his spine straightened.

He rose to his full height, latching a meaty fist around my throat and forcing my back to the wall. His eyes locked down, void of emotion as he leaned closer. His minty breath wafted over my face, and a chill ran down my spine as a sliver of fear crept in. I knew he didn't want to hurt me… but sometimes I wondered how much it would take before he did.

"A month. The first call or text you don't answer, and I am on a flight. Then, with or without this evidence you're sniffing out, I'll rip both fucking families apart." He kissed my temple before pushing against me, storming from the room and slamming the door behind him.

"Every two days, I want a text." Matteo pulled me in for a tight hug. "Keep your head in the game, and don't lose yourself trying to find *him*." He left without another word, and my heart raced as plans continued to turn the cogs of my brain.

New York, here I come, I thought with a devious smile.

Chapter One
PERSEPHONE

The moment I got off the bus from Los Angeles, I knew I'd made the right choice coming back to New York. Hordes of people lost to their own vices—the chaos and noise drove my internal need for calamity. I knew I could do some damage, and the crowds would allow me the anonymity I sought in order to do it.

LA was a sanctuary, offering me the peace and time to heal from my past. I was in no way sane, nor a naturally functioning human being, but I'd made some connections that aided in my survival. Carmine and his family took me under their wing and urged me to seek my vengeance.

He had his own reasons to help, of course. But for once, his reasons had nothing to do with my body. We were playing a game of an eye for an eye. Someone had hurt his family, and they were traipsing in the circles of men who could lead me to my masked captor. It could be a mutually beneficial relationship.

So, I was back in New York and working at a strip club called *Spogliato*. It was clean and high-class, with wealthy and powerful customers. I made some serious cash, which allotted me the ability to continue my mission. This bar just so happened to cater to the elite of the underworld, the rich and corrupt who held the answers I needed.

I chose this place because it was owned by the eldest Moretti son. I planned to use him to get a lead and take him down with the rest of the scum. I just hadn't planned on one thing: the fact that he was pure, raw sex, wrapped up in a pleasing package comparable to that of an Italian god.

Dom Moretti was the picture of control, power, and dirty, dirty sex.

His face was all hard angles, and his body was perfectly sculpted under his button-up shirts; even his suit pants pulled tight to his firm ass. He made me want to crawl on my hands and knees, begging for the smallest taste. He exuded masculinity and discipline, the type of ownership that was capable of harnessing my demons.

One taste, and he turned into an addiction I couldn't shake. His discipline helped me in all the ways I was unable to help myself. Little did I know that the chase for his hard dick would take me down the battered, broken road it did.

Because nothing in my life could ever be simple. Or kind.

The door opened and light poured into the room, forcing me to blink several times. Dom walked inside with all the swagger of a man swinging something heavy between his legs and a million dollars in his pocket—both of which he possessed. Stepping up to my cage, he dropped to a squat in front of me—a silent stare down as I waited for his command.

"Are we ready to try some freedom today?" he asked me, his voice dark and edgy, yet filled with such dominance my body thrummed to life.

"Yes, sir." I grinned back as his eyes filled with suspicion.

I loved to push his buttons. The thrill of my disobedience appeased my inner monster threatening to break loose. He helped me manage the ever-present darkness. Under his command, I could think normally and maintain a semblance of a functioning life—the key that locked my vault and kept the demons at bay. Well, as normal as one could be under the thumb of a trafficker. Yeah, I was the girl on the arm of a man suspected of being the east coast's most powerful skin peddler.

"Get dressed." The harsh scream of the metal bar echoed in my mind.

My room had black walls with a dark red carpet and satin everything—expensive clothing and jewels completed the aesthetic. One side was the wealth he gifted me, the other was the pain and control he brandished.

"Persephone. You try the patience of a saint. Get the fuck in the car," Dom growled from the bottom of the staircase.

I may have been a glutton for punishment, but even I struggled to maintain a calm heart when Dom lost his patience. Sometimes, no matter what I did, it wasn't good enough for him. You see, the man loved two things: influence and… *his sister.* No one could compare to Mirabella Moretti—she practically hung the moon.

It was borderline disconcerting, the way he spoke of her.

The SUV was idling outside of Dom's mansion as I exited the front door. This was my home—at times, my prison—and Dom refused to share me with just anyone. I was his top earner at *Spogliato,* and who he liked to bury himself deep inside of after hours.

"Sit. Now." He pointed to the seat beside him.

"Do you like?" I ask, motioning down the length of my outfit.

My black pencil skirt was tight, showcasing my slender frame. I paired it with a black lace bralette, a white-gold diamond necklace, and his favorite red-soled stilettos. My blonde hair was left long down my back with a slight curl, and my makeup was simple: black eyeliner to accentuate my blue eyes.

"Business casual?" he asked, depositing his phone back into the pocket of his jacket.

My smile was my answer. I shifted slightly, letting the slit of the skirt ride up my thigh while barely covering my panty-less state. His eyes burned with hunger as he watched the movement; his calloused hand grabbed my thigh and squeezed hard enough to bruise. Gripping my chin with the other, he forced me to look into his eyes. The man before me changed in an instant—the hunger replaced with a menacing darkness.

"No panties, hm? Is this your attempt to distract me?" Dom stared into my eyes, not needing my response. "I give you a chance at freedom, and yet you push my semblance of restraint *the moment* I let you out of the house." He growled with such ferocity; my legs slammed together to allay some of my desire.

His palm, still on my thigh, tightened with my movement. His dark brown hair made his smooth olive complexion seem more caramel in color. His honey eyes turned dark—the deepest shade possible. This was the Dom that I craved. I felt whole, not like I was falling apart at the seams.

Licking my lips, I stared back at him—brown eyes to blue—begging him to make a move... taunting him. On a growl, Dom's free hand wrapped around my neck and tugged me closer, while the other continued its impenetrable grip, awkwardly pinning me to the seat. He squeezed my throat, closing off my airways with a delicious tenacity that should cause me pain but instead heightened my desire.

"You see, my little pet, I know your game. You're thinking of all the ways you could be punished, begging me for it. But I let you out of that cage to show you it's time to harness that inner demon." He didn't ease his grip on my throat, my face turning blue as my insides reveled in the delicious torment. "You will behave, then I will deal with you at home."

He released my neck, and I gulped in copious amounts of air. I stared back at him hungrily, my body having released additional endorphins and forcing me to writhe in need. His hand on my thigh pinned me in place as I pleaded to squirm, trying to gain control of myself.

"Fuck it." He growled suddenly, maneuvering me beneath him. "You beg me to punish you when you can't control yourself. Yet, you make me lose *my* control." With a softness I almost didn't believe he could possess, he wiped a stray piece of hair from my face. His hand was still on my neck—holding me down—and his knee was bent on the seat to keep my legs apart.

"I'm sorry," I muttered faintly, my body melting under his strong embrace.

"Don't lie. There isn't a sorry part of that delectable little body. Not now, but there will be when we get home," he promised.

Pulling out his dick—long and heavy—his eyes turned glacial as I licked my lips. He snarled his response as he grabbed his hard length and slammed inside me. I screamed at the contact, my core soaking wet and moving to conform to his size. No matter how many times this man fucked me (we didn't make love, or have sex even; we fucked… and hard) his girth still took me by surprise.

My pristine pencil skirt was shoved up against my stomach— and I'm pretty sure I lost a shoe—as he folded me like a pretzel, fitting awkwardly on the back seat. His large, solid frame assaulted me with thrust after angry thrust, his rage increasing my pleasure and making me teeter on the edge of bliss.

"Don't you fucking come. Not yet, Persephone." His breath came in sharp pants. My body was tempted to disobey and take the final lunge off the cliff of nirvana… but his face warned against it. "Fuck." He brought my leg higher, lifting my ass in the air as he pounded into me, my shoulders imprinting on the seat.

"Oh, fuck." My breathing sounded strange as my body contorted against his maddening assault.

"Now. Fuck. Me. Come." Our shouting as we climaxed together threatened to shatter the windows.

The insanity within my head finally diminished to the point I could breathe again. It was hard to explain, and it never made sense to me until I met Dom. The need for chaos was always lurking under my skin, threatening to break loose, to appease my need for revenge. I couldn't harness my hold on my own sanity, and my mind often sent me to unstable places.

The door on the vault shook as all my secrets swirled inside, chaotic like rain ready to burst from a cloud.

Dom's restraint, his grip on both my metaphorical and physical leash, took that choice away. I couldn't run free without his approval. It was sick—definitely fucked up to admit—but making sense of my reality for other people wasn't my concern.

After years of seeking help, only two things had worked. One: I allowed myself the chance to seek my revenge with no manner of blood spared. Two: Dom's unique ability to harness my inner beast.

"Fuck. Me," Dom muttered, tucking himself back into his pants.

I laughed at him. "Ready so soon?" I twisted in my seat and began adjusting my own clothes.

"Look at me." He grabbed my chin, forcing my gaze to his. I blinked a few times under his scrutiny, feeling my head clear. "There she is." He smiled lightly, kissing my forehead, before he released me and reached down to hand me my discarded heel.

I took a deep breath. I'd been adrift for what felt like days. Dom had brought me to a meeting and I—well, I lost it, destroying their operation from the inside out.

I'd been stuck in my own head since.

"Persephone," Dom barked, snapping me out of my reverie. "Fix yourself and let's go." I adjusted my bralette and made sure my skirt was in place before sliding out of the vehicle.

"Sir." I smirked when Dom checked me out as he turned to the older gentleman.

"Mr. Moretti, nice to see you again." Dom's realtor extended a chubby hand.

"Hello." Dom shook the proffered palm and tugged me behind him when the man went to reach for me. "Shall we?" Dom urged him forward, but I didn't miss the realtor's repugnant glances.

I couldn't help but smile at Dom's actions. I took the stage at *Spogliato* every Friday night, eight o'clock sharp. He'd watch from above the platform in his glass office as I danced for him, pushing his buttons as I crawled across the elevated flooring while allowing men a closer look. It was all a game—the push and pull between us—one neither of us would win if we kept toeing this dangerous line.

The realtor wandered the large warehouse with adjoining offices, going over specs, pricing, and other monotonous details. Dom and his business partner, John, needed a larger space for their enterprise—away from prying eyes.

"Does it have private access to the water anywhere?" I attempted to confirm.

None of it sat right with me, but it wasn't my place.

Dom continued to speak to the salesman, shaking hands before we went our separate ways. I could feel the anger radiating from beside me.

We walked to the waiting SUV, his grip still wrapped around my bicep. I was holding a fist at my side; my jaw was closed tight. I stared at the concrete in front of me to avoid saying anything else. Dom yanked me onto the sidewalk, hiding us behind the idling car.

"What the fuck did I tell you?" Dom growled from within an inch of my face. "I took you out of your cage to test your training. And you, my little pet, you failed… pathetically. I told you I didn't want you involved, and you just had to, didn't you?" He was referring to my question about the water.

I could feel eyes on us. I didn't have to see anyone to know when someone was watching me. Call it a sixth sense I'd picked up when I was a child, but it was always accurate. I'd seen the car pull up across the way, driving into the Agostino-owned lot. I didn't know who *he* was at the moment, but he was watching silently, and it was irritating.

"I didn't do anything wrong." My voice was strong with an undertone of annoyance. But each word was like a slap to Dom's face as he growled in displeasure before throwing me against the car. My svelte frame bounced off the unrelenting metal, flying forward with the impact. Dom grabbed me by the neck and pinned me to the car.

"Nothing wrong?" He snarled in my face, my own agitation instigating a mental shutdown. "Try, you didn't do a fucking-thing-right." He slapped me lightly across the face, snapping me back into the now.

"I'm sorry," I lied. I wasn't sorry, not in the least.

"We all have our roles in this world, Persephone. And if you don't watch your back, I'll change yours very *fucking* quickly." Dom was always ready to remind me, as if I didn't already know. Shoving me away from him, he straightened his tie in the metal's reflection. "Get in the fucking car."

I stumbled backwards as he sat inside and slammed the door. Staying close to the fence posts lining the adjacent property, I addressed our onlooker, still lurking in the shrubbery, before inviting him to the club so I could play with him.

I could sense danger lingering under the skin of that one. Whoever he was, he was loaded with a darkness not much unlike my own, except I let mine out to play in different, *positive* ways.

I positioned myself in the SUV, and it pulled away the moment my door closed. Dom was already on his phone, displeased with whomever was on the other end. "I have more pressing matters than to attend your luncheon. I will come see Bella once my business has concluded," Dom stated angrily to the caller.

"Dom, be there and do not be late. End of discussion." A voice boomed from the receiver.

"We had a guest," I said as soon as the call ended.

"We did, indeed," he confirmed with a sigh, tapping out a text. "Take us to *Vino*," he ordered the driver.

Yeah, he'd seen him too. And we didn't play well with others.

"A sexy luncheon, sir?" I licked my lips in anticipation. His phone rang, stopping him from answering me.

"Hey, unknown suspect overheard Perse and me, nothing meaningful," he said to his partner, John—I presumed. "Okay, I have to meet my father at *Vino*. Yeah, Bella is home." My spine straightened at the mention of the Moretti daughter and her presence back on US soil.

"Am I invited to meet the infamous sister?" I whispered, skimming my fingertips up his thigh to grab his growing erection. His hand struck out—quickly stopping my exploration—his grip tight and painful.

"I will send Persephone home with the car. Can you meet her there and lock her down for me?" he asked John, smirking at my annoyance.

"Fuck." I growled and sunk back down into my seat.

"John will meet you. Be a good girl until I get back." Dom tugged me forward for a chaste kiss, pulling away much too quickly. I grabbed his neck, yanking him back to me while trying to deepen the kiss but he halted the gesture.

"I want you," I whispered, licking his lips and enjoying his taste as it exploded on my tongue.

"My pet, aren't we insatiable today? Have I not given you enough attention?" Dom mocked me with a viciousness.

"Never. And you could give me a little extra since you're sending me to my room like a little kid," I glowered, and his handsome face lit up in response.

"Sorry, my pet, I have things to do and no time for you to be one of them." His laughter only pissed me off more.

"I'm sure it's the first refusal of many to come," I muttered to myself, but Dom heard the off-handed comment, his angered expression thrusting back into my line of sight.

"What's that, pet?" He grabbed my chin roughly. "Don't fuck with me with these little jealous tantrums. Are you forgetting your role here? Do I need to send you away?" The asshole raised his phone in the air.

"Enjoy your lunch," I conceded, staring straight ahead.

"John is waiting for you at home to put you in your cage. I think this freedom today was too much for you." Then the bastard kissed me on the nose before exiting the car. "I'd say behave yourself, but I know you won't. So, Gabriel is here to ensure you make it home." He stepped aside and one of his guards clambered in.

"Seat belt," the guy spat his directive at me as Dom closed the door. When I didn't immediately jump to do his bidding, he abrasively shoved me onto the interior. Reaching across, he tugged on the belt and strapped me in.

I stared out the window, glaring at Dom through the tinted glass as he stood on the sidewalk waiting. The patriarch, Anthony Moretti—I assumed, since I've never met any of Dom's family—emerged from the limo first with his back to me. And next, I suspected, was his eldest son, Gio.

Then I saw her, the woman I'd heard about—incessantly—since Dom first took me. *Mirabella Moretti.*

She had long raven locks that stretched down her back, her body lithe and feminine as she moved in her designer dress and heels. She was gorgeous and twice as sweet—or so I'd been told.

Dom checked up on her while she was away in Italy. Apparently, he was concerned with their father's plans for her future. I felt such pity for the girl, as she'd presumably be married off to someone rich to live the life of a doting housewife!

Insert sarcasm.

We sat there, watching Dom lovingly pull his sister into his embrace. "What the fuck are you waiting for? Go!" I yelled, my babysitter laughing at my expense.

"Jealous?" Gabriel prompted. "She *is* a hot little piece of ass." He gave her a vulgar appraisal before adjusting himself in his seat.

I cackled, observing how he grew uncomfortable when I didn't stop. Dom tapped the window, motioning for the driver to go, as I kept up my hysterics. He didn't look back as he followed his sister inside, no second thoughts about dismissing me.

"Crazy. Fucking. Bitch," Gabriel said, enunciating each word.

I taunted him, reminding him of all the ways Dom would torture him, should he learn of his disrespect towards Mirabella. I couldn't rein in my laughter as I watched the terrifying realization settle over his features. With no preamble, he cocked back a meaty fist—effectively busting open my lip—as he threatened me to silence.

"And now you're a dead man." My laughter continued as I held my head in my hands. I stared at him sideways from under my veil of hair, watching in jubilation as his slow mind wrapped around what happened.

"Not my fault you tried to run away," he ground out, his words dripping with acid.

"Did I, Norm?" I asked the driver, who stared back in the rearview. His head shook in response, much to Gabriel's dismay.

The car pulled up outside of Dom's mansion, and John was standing on the front porch awaiting my arrival. I may have been headed inside to be locked up, but at least I wasn't counting down the hours until my death. Opening my door, John went to help me out of the car but stopped short. My brain was fuzzy, and I couldn't instruct my fingers to unbuckle my belt.

He pulled my hair from my face, as his gentle hands tucked it behind my ear. His eyes switched almost immediately—from kindness to fury—as he took in my appearance. I tried to smile but winced, swallowing back the bile rising in my throat from the force of the impact.

"Norm, do you mind taking Miss Persephone to her room? Please ensure her *cage* is appropriately locked before you leave." He helped me out of the car, handing me off to Norm's soft embrace.

"Easy now," Norm cajoled, guiding me into the house as my temples pounded.

Fucker might have given me a concussion.

My stomach twisted with nausea, and my head was thrumming behind my eyes. We made it into my room—the sounds of the metal scraping against metal alerting me to our entrance—then sweet, sweet darkness took over just as the cold flooring settled into my bones.

Chapter Two
DOMINIC

This woman brought out ravenous emotions within me—often conflicting and dangerous. She made my dick hard and I wanted to suffocate her with it. She was sex and desire, yet the most fucked-up and twisted bitch you'd ever meet.

The look of lust she'd given me as I stepped from the car quickly manifested into jealousy. If it wasn't for seeing my baby sister, I'd tell my father to go fuck himself and show the little green-eyed monster just how hot her possessiveness made me.

My palm twitched, wanting nothing more than to teach Persephone a lesson about talking back. But shit had to be done, and now that Bella was home, I needed *her* to tell me she was okay. She'd grown into a beautiful woman, and I felt even more pressure to protect my little sister.

To protect her from her own family.

She was home just long enough to be auctioned off to the highest bidder. To a mafia son. I needed to make sure my father included her well-being in his decision—while ensuring Gio stayed out of it.

My brother was a loose cannon and an immoral son of a bitch, who would have no qualms about punishing our sister for the hell of it. I had my own way of doing things, and my pops didn't like it; he refused to acknowledge my business. I wasn't an angel, but family came first—Bella and my mother were all that mattered.

I watched the car pull away, my unease rising as it disappeared. I didn't trust anyone. John and I had an exclusive… *partnership*—one that garnered certain benefits and protection. He had a soft spot for Perse, so I knew she was in good hands with him and my driver. Gabriel was to keep her in the car and to get her ass into the house. I wanted to laugh at the look of pure loathing she gave him as I closed the door.

Slowly but surely, Perse was losing her already limited sanity and unraveling. My normal tricks of the trade were only heightening her outbursts. If she didn't straighten her shit out, I'd force John to send her packing. I had a ton of other dancers who could grace my arm and warm my dick. She was here for certain reasons, but soon those reasons would negate any deal I'd made.

I had a feeling she was going to misbehave and several punishments ran through my mind—I smiled to myself. I straightened my spine as my father and asshole brother met with the hostess. We immediately went to the back room, and my steps faltered when I saw Mario Agostino waiting for us.

Bella was past the marrying age in our world, and this luncheon proved the direction the decision was heading. Mario's eldest son, Lucky, was next in line for the throne of New York. On the surface, he was the ideal candidate—someone who could protect her *and* treat her like gold.

Lucky had earned the nickname *il diavolo*, the Italian fucking devil. He was known for many high-profile business deals and had his hand in even more notorious murders. He was the key that ensured his family stayed in power.

The moment the devil himself walked into the room, I knew it. Lucky's father was as cunning as he was powerful—this was his show and we were just the audience. He had a reason for this meeting and I couldn't wait to watch my brother squirm.

Lucky and Gio had an undying hate for each other—my brother wanted New York, but it was Lucky's legacy. Gio was up to something, and whatever it was would *no fucking doubt* cause the family issues. More specifically… Bella.

I grabbed my glass of scotch, and bringing it to my lips, I noticed Persephone's scent lingered on my hand. I shifted in my seat; I could feel myself hardening at the intoxicating aroma. She was goddamn Mata Hari the moment she stepped into my club. At first, I'd refused to give her a job, but the woman was seduction and warmth. She *knew* how to get under my skin, and I *knew* she would be my destruction.

"The girl's got fucking moves," my club manager muttered around his cigarette, blowing the smoke against the glass window.

"The girl is trouble," I said, more to myself. "I don't care how good she is; my gut is telling me no." I crossed my arms over my chest.

"Two shifts—if she's as problematic as you say, she's gone." He laughed at my grumbling.

"Fine. But she is your problem to deal with." I opened the office door and descended the stairs to make my rounds.

Customers acknowledged my presence with a tip of their heads—enough to be respectful, but not so much that it was overbearing. Some dancers took off in fright while others openly flirted. I refused to look at the stage, knowing the girl's set was about to end. The way she moved, her smile, her rapid breath, and the fucking scent of her shampoo made my dick hard.

I didn't need a distraction, no matter how hot she was. Shit with my brother and father had turned sideways, and Pops was planning on calling Bella and Gio home. I'd never gotten along with my father or brother because they didn't give a shit about family—only about themselves and the domination they sought. I was powerful too, but not at the risk of my mother and sister.

I was no saint, but I also had morals when it came to family. They opted to destroy those around them for their own benefit, whereas I fought to protect my mother and sister with everything I had. If that meant others outside of our familial circle had to suffer for my financial gain… well, so be it.

Once I did a final sweep of the club, I headed back towards the staircase that led to my second-floor office. I almost didn't notice until the last minute, but a bulb in the corridor was out. I froze, stepping into the darkness. I pressed my back to the wall and listened.

"Shut up, bitch," a man growled. "You make a fucking sound, and I'll slice your throat."

The tiniest muffled whimper filled the space, and I knew one of my girls was being pinned in the corner. I'd have to check the rotation to see whose post this was, because this was unacceptable. No one touched anything that was mine. If I wanted to send one of these girls to hell, that was my choice. No one else's.

"Do you feel what you do to me? Shaking your ass on that stage for all these men, while knowing you belong to me. The moment I saw you walk in tonight, I knew you were mine." He groaned and a shuffling noise made the girl squeak. "I can't wait to taste your tears and hear your screams. Let's go."

They stepped away from the corner. The large man had a grip on her neck; her blonde hair snaked through his hold. I knew she'd be fucking trouble. *His hand was still around her mouth, but as they turned, I noticed how her eyes grew rounder when she spotted me. The look of fear on her face made me stop in my tracks. Fear. He'd put that there.*

When she'd flounced into my office for her audition, she was cocky—a little spitfire with far-too-much energy and even more sex appeal. Now, I could see she was shaking in fright; her hand was latched onto his grip, and her breasts shook as she tried to fight against his hold.

Not her. Not in my fucking club. Not this motherfucker.

"Did anyone ever tell you it wasn't polite to touch things that didn't belong to you?" I approached him from the rear, my large frame no longer obscured by the shadows.

I wanted to chuckle at the way his spine straightened, how dread trickled through his movements. He knew he fucked up. But I guess he didn't care about the consequences at the time, because he had seen something he wanted. Men were dumb and rash when it came to women, especially an enrapturing temptress like Persephone.

"Mis... Mister Moretti, sir. I..."

I raised my hand to silence him. "You know who I am and where you are." It wasn't a question. "And yet... you thought you could have one of my girls?" I cocked my neck to the side and cracked my knuckles.

"I-I will pay. I... I wanted a closer look before I put a bid in, sir." The stupid motherfucker thought he knew me, knew my business.

The word on the street was I was the go-to man when it came to buying certain… goods. You had a predilection for something specific, and with the right amount of cash, Dominic Moretti could get it for you. They thought I sold girls right off the pole, but why would a legitimate business house illegal activity? Only an idiot would do that.

"You fucking moron." I chuckled, a good wholesome sound that lifted the weight from my chest. "Give her to me."

He shoved her towards me, her thin frame melding into my chest as she shook in fright. I looked down at her—small and frail in my arms—her blue eyes pinned to my chest.

"Don't you fucking move." I growled as the dead man tried turning on his heel. I kept the girl tucked under my arm as I grabbed his neck with the other. "Now, I think it's time we all get better acquainted—you know, see if she is really worth it to you."

At this point, three bouncers had circled us and shielded our exit as I walked towards the basement door. Entering the code, I ushered them down the stairs with a guard at my back. As we hit the halfway mark of our descent, the girl's shakes turned into full-blown hysterics and the dead man started pleading for his life. I could only assume that the smell of bleach, blood, and decay would deter anyone with a weak stomach.

One guard blocked the stairs, as I placed the girl onto the desk against the wall and shoved the idiot towards the middle of the room. He lost his footing and fell, sliding across the tiled floor towards the drain in the center. His pleas grew in pitch as the guard punched him in the gut when he tried rising to his feet. I turned to the girl, noticing she was watching the scene with rapt attention.

"I knew you were going to be trouble," I stated flatly.

For a girl who was shaking in her stripper heels a minute ago, her face was void of emotion as she stared me down. It was like she could see straight through me, like I wasn't even there. She had retreated inside herself, and I would put money on the fact that it was a terrifying place. She was so fragile and lost, a damaged little doll I didn't have time to comfort.

But fuck me, did I want to. I wanted to hold her and take away all the bad the world had given to her. I wanted to shelter her from the terror that I could still see burning bright beneath her irises.

I wasn't a good guy. I hurt people. A lot of people. I wanted to hurt her, but in all the most pleasurably painful ways. I wanted to hear her whimpers when my dick stretched her opening. I wanted to see her eyes blank out when I fucked her raw and choked her into oblivion.

"The question is: are you worth it?" I asked, snapping her from her trance.

"Sir, Mr. Moretti. I…" Her shoulders dropped, and she shook her head. "This time—for once—I didn't cause this." Her voice was flat and calm, her eyes dulled by exhaustion.

"No, I don't believe you did. But, nonetheless, here we are. I will make this right, and I want you out of my club." I held her chin in my hand; she winced when I tightened my grip. "Finish your shift, then you're done."

The words tasted like acid in my mouth. I needed her gone. I didn't want to feel… this. Whatever the fuck she was doing to me, I didn't want it. I wanted her thrown out on her ass, away-the-fuck from me. Even as I said it, my dick hardened, wanting its own taste.

I turned my back on her, nodding towards the bouncer—a silent instruction to remove her from the room. She didn't need to be a witness to what I was about to do. No, she needed to finish her shift and get the hell out of my club—out of my life. John and I were working on something, and she would get in the way.

I got lost in the motions—the repetitive pounding of broken flesh—as I beat sense into the man who would have no use for it. Not anymore. Not how I planned to leave him. I had no idea how long I was down there, but I removed my blood-and-sweat-soaked shirt before climbing the stairs. I needed a shower. And new clothes. So, I darted up the steps leading to my office.

"What the fuck are you doing here?" I growled, a migraine settling behind my eyes when I noticed Persephone sitting on my desk. She smiled at me for a moment before bouncing onto her bare feet.

"Showing my gratitude." Her demented little smirk was back as she flounced towards me. Dropping to her knees, she grabbed my belt.

"This means nothing. Tonight… is still your last night." I grunted, feeling my dick harden.

"Then I better make it good." She reached into my pants and wrapped her slim fingers around my length. I chuckled, enjoying how her eyes widened as she registered my girth.

"Maybe I should ruin you, just to see how pretty your broken pieces are." I growled, grabbing her by the neck and pulling her to her feet. "Your beauty is nothing more than deception at its finest."

That was the moment I should've walked away. I shouldn't have fucked *her on my desk, against the office window, and again in the car on the way home. I shouldn't have started… because after the first hit, the addiction made you forget everything but the next. Yep, I should've fucking sent her packing the moment I sensed the high.*

I held strong for as long as I could. But every man had his weakness and protecting her was mine…

"Repeat. That." I growled into the phone. Saying goodbye to Bella, I hopped into my car.

"Norm locked her down, but she passed out. Gabriel…" John stopped.

"Lock him in the fucking basement. I am on my way," I ordered.

"Dom, I can't allow…"

But I didn't let him finish that thought. There was no need. I knew what he was going to say. "Then get the fuck out of my house if you don't want to be a part of it. He touched what belongs to me, John." I threw my phone against the car door, not caring when the screen cracked.

I sent that motherfucker home with her *to protect her.* I was the only one allowed to break her, because I was the only one who knew how to put her back together. He was a fucking dead man.

I charged into the house, darting towards her bedroom. She was sound asleep, secure in her cage. It was the only time she looked at peace. Whatever storms were thundering in her head, day in and day out, she shut them down when she slept. Usually. Sometimes I woke to her screaming, the sounds resuscitating even the coldest of hearts.

"Hey, baby." I tucked her blonde locks out of her face, smiling as her blue eyes widened at my presence.

"I'm sorry," she muttered, tears tipping over the brims of her lashes.

"Shh. I told you that day we met that I knew you were trouble. But this…" I stopped, taking a deep breath. "This isn't on you. It's on me. I left him with you. Now, get up."

I extended my hand to support her to her feet. She was wearing one of my button-up shirts, the fabric swallowing her whole. There was something territorial inside me that enjoyed seeing her in my clothing. It was a stake of ownership. And I couldn't help but smile.

"Where are we going?" she asked, covering her eyes with her hand and wincing at the light before rubbing her temple.

"I'm apologizing," I said, descending the basement stairs.

"Most girls like flowers and jewelry." She chuckled, wincing again.

"You aren't most girls."

When we reached the bottom, I smiled as Gabriel swayed at eye-level. His arms were bound by ropes above his head, bearing his full weight, as his feet dangled in the air. Norm had done a number on him for me—my driver's concern for Persephone overwhelming his softer nature.

This type of shit wasn't John's forte, which was exactly why he had protested earlier, *and* why we kept him out of it. For numerous reasons.

"For me? You shouldn't have." Persephone tried to act tough, but I could see the pain in her expression.

"*He* shouldn't have." I removed my jacket, wrapping it around her shaking shoulders. Then, I stepped to the table at the side of the room, grabbing a pair of brass knuckles. I wanted to feel the sting of every blow. And there would be many. One after another, I threw punch after punch, enjoying each groan. Each drop of blood. I was lost in the moment, not realizing that my hands were shredded, and he was barely alive.

I turned to Persephone. She was tucked into the corner, on a chair, the wall seemingly the only thing holding her up. She looked like she could be sick at any moment, but I knew it was from the headache and not the violence. Perse had seen a lot of shit in her day; *this* was nothing new.

"Here, baby." I handed her noise-blocking headphones as I pulled my Glock from the back of my waistband.

"Dom." She stopped me from raising my arm. "He also said Bella was a hot piece of ass he wanted to sample."

The little vixen knew just how to set me off. Instead of a bullet to the brain after that beating, I wanted him to suffer a bit longer.

His left knee, then his right. Both elbows. And each shoulder. They all got a round in my sister's honor. I watched him scream in agony. And when he passed out, I woke him up again, letting him relive the pain like a perpetual nightmare without an end.

He should've known better. But sometimes people had to *learn* the hard way. And who was I to refuse a much-needed lesson?

Chapter Three
PERSEPHONE

Warm hands startled me awake, my consciousness plagued by a pounding headache. Slowly, my eyelids unlatched, and I looked around—I was in my room. But I was in my bed with no clue how I got there.

"Hey, beautiful," Dom said softly, looking down at me as he rubbed my arm. "I was wondering when you were going to wake up. How do you feel?" His warm eyes were filled with concern.

"My head is killing me, but I'm okay." I tried to sit up, but Dom held me in place.

The doctor took that moment to walk into my room. As the door was closing, I could see John lurking in the hallway, talking on his phone. My eyes were tested, my blood pressure taken, and all the typical crap doctors loved to do when you just wanted to be left alone.

"She's lost time," Dom told the older man. "Perse, what's the last thing you remember?" They both turned to look at me with expectant eyes.

I tried to think back as far as I could. "Gabriel… he punched me in the face. Norm had to carry me inside." I held my head in my hands, blocking the brightness.

"That's it? Nothing after?" Dom urged. "What about *Hush*?" I stared at him in confusion without a clue as to what he was referring to. Dom and the family-owned physician talked for a few minutes as I closed my eyes and laid my head back.

And then it hit me. I remembered it all: Dom's concern for my well-being. His revenge. I could still smell Gabriel's blood lingering around me… John had updated us with his suspicion that a competitor was traipsing in Dom's city at a local venue.

Hush catered to people with an affinity for expensive spirits and a taste for dirty deeds. I was about to smile when an image of terrifying brown eyes filled my memory.

"We're leaving, Persephone," Dom barked from the threshold in the foyer. Slowly, I shut my door behind me and walked down the corridor. My heels clicking on the marble floor alerted him to my entrance. I was wearing a long black raincoat and black heels—the leather straps tied up and around my calf muscles. My blonde hair was in a high ponytail, the poker straight locks almost reaching my shoulder. My makeup was extra smokey and dark to make my blue eyes pop. "The hell are you wearing?" Dom asked, motioning towards my coat.

"A coat?" I left it as a question, a sensuous smirk on my lips. I loved to rattle his patience because once I removed this top layer, I knew he'd forget his agitation.

His suit pulled tight as he clenched his fists, his large biceps flexing from the movement. John was lingering by the door on his cell phone, but I could tell from his forced cough that he was trying to hide a laugh. He loved our banter, especially when my jokes were at his counterpart's expense.

Dom stepped into my space, grabbing the sash emphasizing my tiny waist, and tugged it open. "Fuck. Me," he muttered, staring at my outfit.

"Do we have time?" I asked, biting my bottom lip.

I was wearing a two-piece leather ensemble and a tiny bra and panty set— black and satin—but the overlay consisted of leather straps covering my chest, torso, and waist. I looked like a bondage present that needed to be unwrapped. Furthermore, black leather was Dom's favorite and the reason he was practically shaking as he slowly lost his bearings.

"We need to leave." John broke the spell that had entranced the two of us, startling me out of my dirty imagination.

"You're no fun, John." I pouted.

"Get in the car," Dom ordered, his jaw clenching tight while breathing deep as he attempted to regain control, before cracking his neck from side to side.

"Yes, sir." I wiggled my eyebrows seductively. I wrapped my coat around my thin frame and practically skipped past him; he responded with a swat to my ass.

"Pull to the employee entrance," Dom instructed Norm.

"Do your thing," John said, smiling at Dom's possessive growl.

Opening the door, I went to slide out, but Dom's rough grip held on to my wrist. "Behave. Got it?"

I nodded but his knowing gaze assessed the labored breaths now parting my lips. He let go of my hand, and I half stumbled from the car, turning quickly and heading to the building. I was lost in the motions once I entered the club, my brain on autopilot as I searched the crowd.

The girl at the front desk paged the waitress stand, as I grabbed the items the newly arriving patron requested. I prepared a bottle, ice, and glasses with a nasty cigar. Once my tray was in place, I set out to greet the customer. Heading towards the designated suite, I swayed my hips to the rhythm of the song.

When the towering figure stepped into the room, his large frame almost had to turn sideways to fit. He was well over six feet tall and wide with bulky muscle. Every inch that was visible in his tailored suit was covered in intricate tattoos. This hot-as-fuck man was chaos wrapped in a five-thousand-dollar suit.

Did the temperature in the room spike or was that my pussy talking?

His spicy cologne and raw masculine scent consumed me as he passed, enticing my interest even further. He surveyed me with an electrical current that I could practically feel burning the parts of my skin he was devouring with his eyes.

I needed to leave, to run for my fucking life. I already had one possessive alpha trying to dictate my narrative. I didn't need another. And this one… this one I could tell… I'd never survive him. Before I could flee, he stopped me. His skin on mine was like touching a burning stovetop. I knew I needed to pull my hand away, but my brain couldn't follow through.

And then his face clicked. He wasn't locked in my memory, my vault, from a previous interaction but from my research. Apollo Deluca, right hand to the future mafia leader of New York—Lucifer, il diavolo, Agostino. Fuck, I didn't need this type of attention.

He held on to my arm in silence, and I knew it was because he wanted to sample a taste… of me. And that wasn't happening. "I only dance, sir." He threw several hundred-dollar bills onto the table, motioning towards the elevated platform.

My first song was a slow rhythm so I could lead into my pole work, methodically making my way to the top near the ceiling. Just as the beat picked up and the song went into a crescendo, I dropped headfirst to the floor. Catching myself and rounding off with a handstand, I then slid to my stomach to roll into my signature move. I crawled towards the end of the stage. Holding it tightly, my head went over the edge between his legs and I flipped into his lap. I clung to his neck as I ground down, enjoying the hardened merriment I was eliciting.

I let his hands roam and explore my body; his rough, calloused touch tickled my smooth skin—until he tried taking my masquerade mask off. I lifted my ass and plopped it onto his lap rougher than necessary. His growl was a mixture of slight discomfort and a need for aggression.

I left quickly and shut the door behind me. Navigating the main room, I saw Dom and John enter. I could still feel Dom's grasp on me as he watched my every move. I blew him an exaggerated kiss before setting my plan into motion.

I wandered the room—smiling at different patrons—all the while scouring for my next target. The thrill, the adrenaline, and the hope of righting a wrong was a heady combination that surged me forward. My brain worked quickly, memorizing each face as I passed; the vault had locked in his long ago. I knew, no matter how he tried to hide, I would recognize him.

And then, as if God answered my silent prayer, there he was.

Jacob Whitman: it sounded like a strong, proper name, belonging to a wholesome young man. But that was a stark contrast to the son of a bitch in front of me. He was overweight by almost a hundred pounds, and his lack of hygiene was nauseating; his acrid smell hit my nostrils from across the room. My hands tingled and my heart slowed as I watched him talk and laugh.

He glanced in my direction—no doubt feeling my eyes assaulting the back of his head—but his leer wasn't one of recognition, just longing. He didn't remember me. Part of me was happy while another part was annoyed. He was one of the buyers when I was taken, forever etched in my psyche.

"Breathe deep," Dom whispered in my ear, suddenly embracing me as he stood protectively at my back. "We've got him. Don't let him smell your fear."

"I'm not afraid. I'm fucking angry." I growled, my body shaking with the memories.

"Good. Anger is good. Look, John sees him; this is his last breath," Dom continued, just as John jumped from his table and lunged for the fat piece of shit.

Men started shouting, tables flipped, guns were cocked, and girls screamed. The melee that pursued pushed me forward, my initial rage boiling over the surface and transitioning into bloodlust. That motherfucker was mine.

I shoved out of Dom's grasp, charging across the space while ignoring everything else in the room except my target. Except Jacob. I had eyes only for him—he would go down by my hands. The room erupted in further chaos as armed FBI agents stormed the facility and started grabbing Jacob's crew.

Somehow, in the mess of it all, my target had managed to sneak across to the other side of the room to flee. Turning on my heels, I charged after him until large hands wrapped around my torso. I fought with everything I had, but I could hear John barking commands in my ear while holding my body tight to him.

It was a battle I knew I wasn't going to win, but I'd be damned if I was going to make it easy for him. As the crowds started clearing the room and fighting with security, Dom charged towards me. I pointed and yelled at Jacob's retreating form, but Dom didn't care about anything other than me. Twisting my head, I saw Jacob rushing towards Apollo and recognized the beast at his side: Carmine Ragetti.

As quickly as Carmine glanced at me, I watched him stare at my intended mark—the coward's portly body was slamming through tables to get to his freedom, but it was short lived. Moving swiftly, with a natural flow of movements only hardened killers could possess, Apollo and Carmine plunged their knives into Jacob. His weighted body dropped to the floor with such force I could hear it over the shouting.

Dom and John tugged me out the back door, down the alley, and into the waiting car. They were both breathing heavy from the exertion, their suits coated with a splattering of blood. As the adrenaline slowly dissipated, I could feel my mind shutting down to protect itself.

"Perse, stay with me." I could hear Dom's command, but it was all too much.

Opening my eyes, I jolted out of the memory as I stared at everyone in the room. Dom was glaring back with his normal hardened, blank expression. The doctor was at my side, making notes on his pad, and John was floating behind them. I cleared my throat and told them I remembered everything.

"He's dead and most of his higher-ranking men were picked up by the FBI," Dom said, rubbing my thigh with a tenderness I couldn't fathom.

"It's over, P," John offered from a distance, a sad smile on his face. "My connections found fifty-two kids in a hidden location off the northern port."

"They're safe," I said, and it wasn't a question. I knew John would ensure all the children were returned home or placed into the best possible care. "He's shut down for good?"

"Yeah, Perse." Dom smiled. "I know you'll never forget your past, but you saved a lot of kids from that same nightmare." *Kids were off-limits.*

"He was a big fish in a fucked-up pond," John muttered, sitting in the chair next to my bed.

That was the thing: I didn't want one or two guys. I wanted their bosses. I wanted to destroy everyone from the top down, to dismantle the kingpins who hurt the innocent. I didn't want it for myself. I wanted it for the others who wouldn't escape like I had. Or those who would escape the physical prison, but never the confines of their own minds. And the man in front of me... Dominic Moretti. He was the last name on my list.

"I didn't even get to play with my food; it was total bullshit. So, who's next?" I asked, my palms itching for more destruction.

"Chill out, little one." John headed for the door.

"You only have one job right now, pet," Dom said, his eyes filling with desire. I licked my lips and sat up in bed, liking where this was headed. "You need to get ready. It's Friday." I groaned in acknowledgment, before flopping onto the bed dramatically.

Dom said goodbye to the doctor and strolled to the door behind John. I rose from the bed, quietly creeping towards the threshold, in an attempt to eavesdrop.

"Do you have any more information on your brother?" John was speaking to Dom.

"Not yet. Gio is being tight-lipped, but he isn't smart enough." Dom's voice dripped with annoyance.

"His involvement with the Russians is going to backfire. I suggest having an exit strategy for yourself." The threat hung in the air and I was unsettled by it.

"I don't know what's up his sleeve, but I'm sure he plans to use the Russians to take on Lucky. And he's going to lose. Again." *Now, that was interesting.*

True to their core, if the Italians had issues within their ranks or with rival families, they handled it themselves. They kept things amongst their kind, and involving the Russians was a direct insult. If they found out what Gio was doing, the Agostinos would destroy him. And because Dom was a Moretti, he could be collateral damage.

"My sister is marrying Lucky; she might be my only saving grace," Dom said, his impatience clear.

"They announced it?" John asked, surprised.

"Not officially, but my mother told me. She's hoping it'll keep her and Bella safe from Pops and Gio's schemes."

"Do we have any news on your father?" John prompted as their footsteps sounded in the distance. "I know he'd never accept working with the Russians; he's too proud."

"At this point, if it lined his pockets, I don't doubt he'd be involved. He raised Gio, after all. It's because of his *lessons* that my brother has this chip on his shoulder."

"What about using Persephone?"

"Only if it comes to that, then I'll send her into my parents' house. As a maid or something. Let her snoop around." Dom's suggestion grated on my nerves.

Of course he wanted me to play the maid, and I'd bet the outfit would be inappropriate—fuck, just the thought of playing another game turned me on. The bastard knew just what strings to pull with me.

"Let me call my connections… see if they can figure out where the money is suddenly coming from." And then there was silence.

Gio and Anthony Moretti were up to something. My heart raced, and my mind churned as I tried to think about what it all could mean. It was so much more than just working with the Russians. Everything inside me told me that much.

A sixth sense—a foreboding—was settling in my stomach at the thought. The two didn't have the best relationship, so Dom would really have to turn up the acting chops to get on his old man's good side. It would be the only way for him to alleviate his father's misgivings.

But something didn't make sense… Anthony Moretti paid money to use the Agostino docks and seemed to be at Mario's mercy. It was clear Gio wanted to ruin Lucky… but why was his father playing bitch to Mario? I had a feeling I knew the answer, and that meant I needed to update Carmine.

I stepped away from the door and started packing for my set at *Spogliato* tonight. My usual sense of indifference for dancing was suddenly replaced with excitement, and I had no idea why. But there was work to do, and I was just the girl to own that stage.

Chapter Four
PERSEPHONE

The bass from the music below Dom's office shook the floor with the slightest vibration. Looking out the window positioned above the stages, I watched the club begin to fill—eight o'clock rearing its ugly head. I wasn't so cocky to say they were all here for me, but I was honest enough to admit the majority were.

I was damn good at what I did. I was a mess of torment, sexuality, and chaos on the inside—but the outside was an image of picture-perfect rhythm that put professional seductresses to shame. Either way, on that stage, I was untouchable.

I smirked at the men entering… and the women flocking to empty their all-too-eager wallets. It was like a drug, and I was obsessed with getting high. Owning men who acted like they were superior, but in reality, were falling victim to a fantasy—a fantasy we created for them.

"Well, that's a new outfit." Dom walked up behind me, pressing his erection into my back and showing me his appreciation for my selection.

I wasn't allowed to do private dances, so my sets were normally a minimum of five songs—a layer of clothing removed with each. As I watched the crowd, I stood in my final ensemble. Dom's rapt attention made me glad I had opted to wait a little longer to get dressed.

My finale outfit was white; the strings and sequins glowed in the blacklights of the club. They gave me an appearance of a natural tan, making my blonde hair and blue eyes shine all their own. The thong rested against my hip bones, adding to the voluptuous shape of my rear. My perky breasts were cupped by the small bra that was mostly sheer, except for the hearts covering my nipples. White bands sat high at the tops of my thighs—elevating my ass—with white straps wrapped around my long legs, ending with a bow and my clear stilettos.

"You make me lose control." Dom snaked his hands around my stomach and pulled me flush against him, my back to his chest. "You haunt my thoughts every waking moment you aren't beside me."

Even in high heels he was taller than me, his hard length digging into my lower back. He pulled my long curls off my shoulder and sniffed below my ear, before placing a soft kiss in *that* perfect spot. And I moaned. His answering growl sent goosebumps down my spine as he bit my neck.

"I need you," I whispered the plea, hating how weak he made me. Hating how much I needed him, in order to feel alive.

"Show me." He pulled away so quickly I had to catch myself. Walking over to his desk, he twirled his chair away from it. His eyes blazed with hunger and lust; the look had my pussy clenching with anticipation. Flipping a switch, he smirked as music filled his office.

My hips swayed rhythmically while I approached him, feeling the beat as my hands traced my body, drawing his attention to each grope and pluck of my fingers. Normally my seduction was method-ical. Slow. Not tonight. I was wound too tight.

I dropped to straddle him in the chair, plopping down hard on his lap exactly how I knew he preferred. Nothing with us was ever sweet and soft, both of us enlivening with the pain. That was why we matched each other so perfectly: He was a mess of rage and dominance, molten lava simmering under the surface. And I was a mess of uncontrollable errant thoughts and chaotic actions—my insides pleaded for his ability to satiate my tumultuous appetite.

Forever a fire burning that only Dom seemed able to appease. As I rode him hard, in tune to the music, his snarl flashed before he shoved me backwards. He picked me up in one strong motion and placed me on his desk. Painfully slow, he pulled my white thong down my legs, leaving me in my heels and garter straps.

Opening my thighs, he sat back and stared at my swollen entrance, glistening and ready for him to take me hard and fast. His face was overloaded with desire as he shoved my thighs as wide as they would go. He unzipped his pants and pulled out his long, thick cock—letting it sit heavy in his hands while stroking himself.

"Come for me." He motioned for me to play with myself as he watched. This was my least favorite game, and he knew it. But it also added to the confirmation of his ownership. When I didn't immediately move, he asked, "Well, pet?"

My right hand dropped from my thigh, finding my core soaked and hot from his perusal. Rubbing myself, gently at first, I twitched as I hit the bundle of nerves begging for torture. I pinched my nipple through my bra with my left hand as my right began chasing the orgasm that was so close—yet seemed a million miles away.

"Come for me, Perse," he ordered again, and my entire body shook with the demand. I panted and increased my speed, but I couldn't come. His knowing smirk pissed me off as he rose to his feet. "You can't, can you? That's right: I own your pleasure."

"Please, sir," I begged before he grabbed my shoulders and twisted me on his desk.

I landed with my head upside down, hanging over the ledge while staring at his hard dick. I opened my mouth; he didn't need more of an invitation and slowly inserted himself—his taste exploding on my tongue. It was slow and soft, until he found his usual punishing speed. In and out, he hit the end of my throat and immediately pulled back. His right hand went to my neck as he pumped his hips, squeezing just enough to add to the thrill of the motions, while his left reached across my body and began playing with my overly sensitized clit.

I was on the cusp of an earth-shattering orgasm, but I needed more. Dom could read my mind. He tightened his grip at the same time he pinched my swollen clit. The sharp pain and lack of air sent my body into a spiral of pure bliss, my muscles constricting in the midst of complete nirvana. He let go and pulled himself out of my mouth. Walking around the desk, he stopped between my legs.

I watched him with lazy eyes, his stare making me pant. His head dropped between my thighs as he tasted the orgasm he'd forced out of me—licking and sucking lightly—his face glistening as he attacked my core like a man starved.

"Feel it, Persephone. Take it," he ordered. Two more orgasms, and my mind was hazy. And that's what Dom did: he took what he wanted and my traitorous body followed his commands. He gripped my thighs and tugged me towards the edge of the desk.

Without warning, he slammed forward, freezing when he buried himself deep inside me. "I want them to smell the sex dripping off you. Smell me on your skin. Show them I fucking own you." He started moving, pounding into me so hard my breathing faltered, and another lingering orgasm started building. "Tell me you're mine!"

"Yes! I'm yours!" I yelled just as my orgasm reached its peak. Consuming me. Devouring me. My mind and body reeled as he reached his own release.

"Damn right you are, pet." He kissed me sweetly and helped me to my feet. I stepped towards the bathroom to clean up, but his hand on my wrist stopped me. "Leave it. I wasn't kidding when I said I wanted my scent on you."

He dropped to a knee in front of me, and holding out my white thong, he guided my legs into the material. Slowly, he lifted the straps up my thighs and into place. He caressed along my slit, making me tremble.

I dressed in a peacoat with a white shirt and tight skirt, before heading to the lower level. The place was packed as I climbed the stairs and roamed the stage, much to my customers' delight. Suddenly, the hair on the back of my neck stood up as I watched a large shadow walk through the crowd and sit at the elevated VIP booth.

A cloud of foreboding seemed to circle him as he moved through the crowd; patrons practically jumped out of his path. He wore a dark suit with a deep-red shirt, which remained open at the collar; his tattoos gave him away. I was practically purring as I crawled to the edge of the stage—much like our prior interlude—to get a better look.

It was the man I danced for at Hush. Apollo-fucking-Deluca.

Sharp honey-brown eyes watched me with treacherous intent, eliciting a shiver down my spine. I liked danger and it poured off this man in waves of destruction and despair. I strutted towards him and watched as his jaw tightened; he stared me down with a blank yet psychotic expression.

I glanced up and saw Dom standing at the window, watching the platform as usual. Except, this time, his concentration wasn't on me. Even from this distance, I could see his anger, before he quickly disappeared from view.

I moved around the stage, humming my siren call and garnering all the attention in the room. As the songs changed, my clothes dwindled and my pole tricks became more daring. So lost in my performance, I noticed too late that Dom was in the back of the club with Apollo.

Their discussion was heated. Dom's entire body was tense, prepared to attack. My view was blocked as another patron walked in front of them, his large frame stealing my gaze.

"Fuck." My groan was muted by the music.

The tall, imposing man moved lithely and with all the swagger of a tiger ready to strike. The fact that *he* was here meant that my lack of prompt responses had worn on his limited patience.

Once off the stage, I was escorted into the dressing room by security before immediately heading into the showers. Changing into a pair of yoga pants and a sports bra, I stepped into sneakers and checked the hallway. Security was standing at each end, barring my exit.

"Hey, I need your help." I held up a fifty-dollar bill to the blonde dancer. "Can you stall security for me?"

The girl was impossibly tall in her thigh-high boots—a perfect fit for her dominatrix act. She gave me a wink, straightened her tits that were wedged into the leather corset, and snatched the bill from my hand.

I moved quickly down the other hall and stepped into the kitchen. No one said anything to me as I snuck out the back door. The overhead light looming against the fence line burned bright, shadowing Carmine's face while heightening his intimidating stature.

"I told you… you can't come here," I said, trying to sound agitated in order to mask my uncertainty.

"And I told you… I wanted information." He lit up a cigarette. "You didn't call."

"Because I don't have anything yet." I crossed my arms over my chest; his eyes took in the motion as my breasts lifted.

"I somehow doubt that." He blew smoke at me, stepping into my personal space. "I'd hate to have to hurt this pretty face."

"I'm close to getting answers. I'll have your proof soon." I stared up at him defiantly. "And don't come back here. Dom won't like seeing you. The other night was already a close call."

He let out a deep, masculine laugh. "Does it look like I give a fuck, Seph? Dom and that whole fucking family are lucky they're still breathing." He stomped the cigarette out with his boot.

"You can't touch them." I swallowed back my panic.

"Tell me, Seph. Why're you so upset?" He stepped even closer, grabbing my chin with unnecessary force.

"Carmine," I whispered, suddenly exhausted.

"Don't let him get in your head. You're not just here to ride his dick." He scowled. "What if he's involved? Have you thought about what that means?"

"I don't know what you're talking about," I muttered, holding his gaze.

"Sure you don't. Don't look crazy in the eye and say you ain't crazy. 'Cause, baby, you're as fucking crazy as I am." He turned away from me, heading towards the parking lot. "You're out of time. I'm about to start a fucking war, and I'll kill anyone in my goddamn way." He threw the words over his shoulder, like a slap to my face. "My promise to find you answers is the only thing keeping them alive… for now."

He must have been preparing to succeed his father, wanting to clean up loose ends before taking the patriarch down—which meant avenging his uncle. All fingers pointed at Anthony Moretti, but Dom was a card I hadn't anticipated drawing.

Carmine was right. It didn't matter that Dom gave me an escape from my own daunting mind. He was the son of the potential enemy. I couldn't keep up this charade much longer. I needed to get my head right.

I crept back inside, beelining for Dom's office, with the guard suddenly on my tail. Smiling at a few leering customers, I didn't stop when they grabbed my hand—security barking at them to back off. As I approached the hallway, I saw Dom was still arguing with Apollo.

"Lucky will protect her with his life, as will the rest of the family." Apollo's declaration had my steps faltering.

"You fucking better believe I'll make sure of that." Dom then turned his full attention to me, pulling me close. "As for Gio, I don't know what he has his hands in, but I plan to fucking find out."

"Be sure you do that." My breath caught in my throat as Apollo's eyes plowed into mine, and I instantly felt naked, my layers pulled back by his intense scrutiny.

"Yeah. Now get the fuck out of my club." Dom pulled me under his arm—an act so innocent, now painted a target on my back. However, the possessiveness made my heart skip a beat and I had to internally chastise myself. "Come on, baby."

Apollo didn't say anything else, but his attention was terrifying. I needed to complete my job and get the fuck out of this city before it was too late.

Before I was broken beyond reparation.

Chapter Five
DOMINIC

"Thank you, Norm. Get her home, and I will be there soon." I kissed the tip of Persephone's nose, watching them pull away from my club.

Fuck, the shit she does to me. After being so enraged by Apollo in my club, her sweet pussy was the best thing to calm me down. The night was beginning to dwindle but I had a few *other* things I needed to focus on. Darting up the stairs, I slammed the office door closed behind me.

"Working with the enemy, baby brother?" The voice echoed from across the room, accompanied by the spin of my office chair.

"What the fuck are you doing here, Gio?" I asked, ripping my suit jacket off.

"Just checking in on my little brother. Is that so wrong?" His stupid grin was about to earn a fist.

"Cut the bullshit," I demanded.

He kicked his heels off my desk and sat forward. "It's time to deal with the Agostinos." His tone was calm, calculated. And not at all like *him*. "Pop's a fucking pussy, bowing down and taking it up the ass. Now he wants to hand Bella over to that *cazzo di figa*."

"Lucky would protect her with his life," I argued.

"And that's enough? She'll be his *whore*; she'll be fucking scum just like them." Venom dripped from his words.

"And you have someone better in mind?" I laughed, unbuttoning the top of my shirt. When he didn't answer, I noticed his smirk. "Who?"

"Someone who will create a better alliance than some small-time fucking *wop* from New York." He sat back, pressing his hands together, seemingly pleased.

"What the fuck are you doing with the Russians, Gio?" I had no idea who the man in front of me was. My idiot, hotheaded brother was long gone, while this version was unrecognizable.

"I'm not stopping at New York. I want it all."

"What have you done?" My anger consumed me as I charged towards the desk.

Stepping around it, he leaned into me. "Careful, Dom. Or I'll give you a matching scar." He reached out towards my chest, but I slapped his hand away.

He didn't have to touch it. Just mentioning the incident set my skin on fire. The mark smoldered under my shirt, the raised skin that ran from shoulder to shoulder itching as if it had scabbed over yesterday. I was just a fucking teenager—barely understood what it meant to be a *made man*. Something that, to this day, I still didn't want. But I was forced into this world with a 9mm pressed to my hand and an unfathomable decision to make: them or me.

"Keep that in mind, baby brother." He stepped away. "I might stop back for that hot little blonde." He closed the door and descended the stairs.

I picked up my chair and chucked it against the wall, my chest heaving. My clothes suddenly felt too tight. I ripped my shirt off, tossed it on the floor, and watched from the window as he disappeared out the front door.

I couldn't catch my breath as I stormed around the room, tugging my hair. As much as I wanted to forget that day, the scar on my chest was excruciating and the memories more so.

"There can only be one heir. Gio, it's your right because you're the oldest,"

my father said, and my brother turned to sneer at me. "When you get the throne, you need to protect it from everyone."

I didn't care what the hell he was talking about. My father liked to go on these long tangents about power and how our family name should be feared.

I just wanted to go inside and have the chef make Bella and me some sand-wiches. We'd been playing outside all day, having fun, until I was forced to come inside and listen to this crap.

"I will run this city. Not Lucky. Not his family." Gio's fists tightened, shaking at his sides.

"Can I go now?" I asked.

Quickly, I realized it was a mistake as they both turned to glare at me. They knew how I felt about our family and this supposed power. I had my own destiny; I just didn't know what it was yet. But everything within me knew it wasn't... this.

"Dominic, do you think all of this was handed to me?" My dad pointed around the large office. "I suffered, I slaved, and I committed sins that would make the devil blush. All, so my coward-of-a-fucking-son could beg to go play *with his* sister.*" He spat at me.*

Gio's face lit up. He loved when my dad ripped me apart. My brother could keep the throne, and I'd happily fuck off. But no. Gio always had to play games; he was unhinged and would do whatever it took to get what he wanted—family be damned.

"I understand: Gio is the oldest... he gets the throne." I tried shaking off his words, but they still burned. "I'll leave you two alone."

"Look, Pops. Dom's going to suck on mom's titty and probably play with Bella's dolls," Gio taunted.

Even though I knew it would end badly—that I should let it go—I turned on my heel and charged for him. My father erupted in laughter, urging us to rip each other's throats out. We grappled back and forth, both swinging but barely making contact.

"Pop said Bella will be our keys to the kingdom." Gio chuckled. "Sell that little bitch to the highest bidder and finally be rid of her. Like they should've done to you!"

I landed two solid punches to his face before he got back to his feet. We circled each other, but I noticed the crazed look that took over as he licked his bloody lip—my father was laughing and shouting, wanting more to spill.

He was in the mafia, a bad man making bad decisions. But the mafia was supposed to be about family, and family was supposed to be everything. And yet, they wanted to destroy ours for their own gain.

"You don't have the fucking balls to do what needs to be done." Gio's right fist caught me across the chin. "We're the fucking Morettis. We make our own way, and fuck anyone who stands in it."

"You're willing to give up your own sister for that?" I asked, taking another hit to the face and one to the stomach.

"I will make sure Bella is taken care of when we decide where she goes. Don't worry. But she is just a woman." He shrugged.

That's what our father had taught us—that men were superior. But after all he had done to get our mother's hand, it didn't make sense. Then it clicked: he showed power by taking her. From another man. And another family.

My mother and sister didn't matter. To them.

"And that's enough for you! She's our sister!" Left, right, left. I came at him swinging hard. "You're fucking disgusting! You're nothing! Always gonna be nothing."

The moment it left my mouth, I knew it was a huge mistake. The cloud of anger that settled over him turned him into someone I didn't recognize. He had a renewed surge of energy, coming at me with everything he had.

My vision was blurred, and everything hurt as I rolled onto my back before staring up at two shadows. I knew they were my father and brother, but neither of them made a move to help me as I whined in pain. My stomach twisted in agony and I felt vomit churning in the back of my throat.

"Are you going to make sacrifices to ensure this family succeeds?"

I rolled onto my side, my shirt sticking to my sweaty skin. I rose to my feet, pulled the wet material over my head, and threw it on the floor. I was winded, but I had to keep moving, or I feared they would kill me.

He was going to win; he was twice my size already. I'd barely started filling out, too thin for my height. Not to mention, the explosive mixture of rage and insanity, which threatened to tear my brother apart from the inside out.

"Come on." I grunted, waving my hands as I got into a fighting stance.

"Wow, the boy has some balls after all. See, Gio. He does have some fight." My father clapped my shoulder before exiting the room.

I smiled, wincing at my split lip as he left, and dropped my hands. My father always pitted us against each other, offering me a semblance of pride while challenging Gio. I didn't know what it was, but he held this impossible standard for my older brother. And the bastard hated me for it.

The door closed, and I turned to look at Gio. But he wasn't across the room anymore—he was charging for me. I had no time to react before he was in my face, a calm and eerie expression on his, as he raised his right hand in the air.

Only then did I notice the knife.

It was too late. I couldn't protect myself or stop it from happening. I didn't feel it at first, didn't register the fire searing across my chest as the skin tore. The pain came minutes later as I stared at the blood pouring down my stomach. I gasped for air while yelling through the agony.

"Where are those balls now?"

I stared up at him, wondering where my brother had gone. "Why? We're fam... family." My limbs were weakening. Limp. Cold.

"Oh, please. Pop is begging to suck Mario Agostino's cock because he's pathetic. He's making a mockery of us. Stay out of my way, little brother, or you'll end up on the wrong end of my blade." He dropped the blood-covered knife next to me. "Again." Then, he walked away, leaving me writhing on the floor.

"Where's Dom?" I could hear Bella's sweet little voice on the other side of the door.

No! Don't let her see this!

"Stay out of Pop's study! He went upstairs, you little brat." I coughed, relieved that he'd forced her away. "Mom, Dom needs you in the study!"

"Yes, baby." I heard the hinges creak open and my mom walk into the room. "Oh my God! Dominic!"

A single tear ran down my cheek, but I was crying for so many reasons. I was crying for my beautiful mother, who was forced to marry a man like my father and bear a son like Gio. For my little sister, who I would fight tooth and nail to protect from her own family. And I cried for myself. For the kid dying on the floor. The kid who, should he survive, would never be the same again.

"Oh God, you scared me." I woke up to my mother crying over the railing of my hospital bed. It took twenty-five stitches and a lot of blood to piece me back together. "Tell me who did this, baby."

"Mom, I need your help." She leaned closer, and I knew she was the only one who would understand. "I need to talk to Mario Agostino."

She didn't even try to hide the fact that she was still in contact with him. I knew they were in love when they were younger, but they were both betrothed to other people. They'd stayed close—behind my father's back—but Mario always checked on her. So, when she called him and told him to come to my hospital room, he came.

"Your mother said you wanted to speak to me." Mario Agostino was intimidating, his large body blocking the overhead light. "You going to tell me who did this to you?"

"No. I'll handle that myself." He stared at my weak body with doubt. "Not right now, but they will get theirs. I wanted to speak to you… about Bella."

"I'm listening." He crossed his arms over his chest.

"She isn't safe here. She's too sweet for our world. I need you to protect her." He looked at my mother through the window.

"If I take her, it will start a war." My head dropped on the pillow. "But I do have an ace up my sleeve—one I've been saving. For your mother, I will do this. I will save Bella."

"She can't stay here, can't stay near my family." I panicked, coughing as my chest burned.

"I have relatives in Italy. Manarola, to be exact." He stared into the distance, glacial and foreboding. "I'll handle your father." His eyes lit up with greed and something else… something sinister.

I knew he was a master manipulator, a forward planner. You didn't get to where he was without having to scheme. To think ahead. But my young mind had no idea just how much would be set into motion with a simple request, made by a little kid, who was only trying to protect his sister.

I ran a heavy hand over the wound, still remembering the sting and pull of the stitches. That was the day that cemented my future. I wasn't going to be that weak little kid ever again. I entered that hospital a broken boy and left a hardened man—a predator.

My brother wanted to destroy the Agostinos, but it wasn't until then that I realized what measures he'd take, in order to succeed. I did what I could to prepare myself for the war my brother and father were starting. But things since then settled to a slow boil as they waited for the *right time*. I had no idea what was up their sleeves, but like I told Apollo: I'd fucking find out.

I created my empire of money, power, and influence to combat whatever they set into motion. I had an arsenal of people and protection at my disposal. Too many people with too many secrets.

Dirty secrets. The kind they'd die to keep hidden. Or kill to keep buried. There was no better incentive to fight by my side than complete and utter ruin.

My muscles began to twitch. I was losing control of my emotions—something that clouded my logic. The wound on my chest felt as fresh as the one inside it. My heart was racing, my breathing labored. I needed to redirect my energy.

And there was only one solution when I was out of my mind.

The car had barely stopped when I jumped out, my feet pounding on the walkway. The house was quiet; most of the staff were gone for the night. Light streamed from the small opening of her door, her scent calling to me.

I slammed forward, the heavy wood bouncing against the wall— she barely noticed. She was brushing her hair as I approached, but the look in her eyes made me falter.

She was gone. The blues of her irises were glassy and distant. She was lost in her mind and the trauma was reflecting back at me. She needed me just as much as I needed her. I yearned to maintain control, and she never hesitated to jump at my command.

Our *relationship* was mutually beneficial, each seeking solace in the other. She couldn't focus unless she was pulled from her misery and told how to function. It wasn't perfect. Fuck, it was certifiable. But it worked for us.

Stopping two feet in front of her, I snapped my fingers, forcing her to jolt upright in her seat and stare back at me. I waved my hand, pointing at the floor by my feet. And like a good little girl, she moved without hesitation.

Her chin dropped to her chest as she stood before me, her white gown doing little to hide her rosy nipples. Using my pointer finger, I lifted her face to look at me. Her eyes were round and filled with such torment. I wanted to eviscerate whoever put that look there.

She was mine. Who knew for how long? But she belonged to me until then. She shook her head and her eyes cleared, challenge replacing the anguish. On a growl, I wrapped my hand around her throat and squeezed, before walking her backwards until she hit the wall with a resounding thud.

"You want to play, is that it?" I asked, closing off her airway so she couldn't answer. "Then let's play. Knees… now."

And she obeyed. No reluctance. No talking back. She was my good little pet. And I couldn't wait to see how far I could push her until she had nothing left to give me. I sneered in her direction as she sat on her heels and waited for my next command.

"Take it out. It won't suck itself," I grunted the order.

I closed my eyes and let her mouth alleviate the bullshit. I locked my mind away from my family drama. The pain vanished from my chest, and she sucked out all of my demons with the knowledge I'd soon vanquish hers too.

Chapter Six
PERSEPHONE

A couple of days later, I was dropped off for a *doctor's* appointment. Norm left me at the door and Dom's guard stayed in the waiting room. The nurse's eyes were filled with fear as she opened an exam room door, then ran away like hell was on her heels.

"Panties off. Knees up and spread 'em. You know the deal." Carmine gloated, snapping a plastic glove on his hand for good measure.

"Yeah-yeah." I tossed my purse into the chair and kicked off my heels as I climbed onto the table. "What do you got?" I tucked my legs to my chest, wrapping my arms around them.

"Someone is fucking with Lucky's shipments and he knows Gio is somehow involved." Carmine picked up a tongue depressor, slapping it against his palm.

Putting my head to my knees, I nodded. "The Agostinos have a rat feeding information to Gio. I don't think they know Gio and Yuri are working together."

Yuri Bucharov was a fucking nobody, trying to act like he was part of the Russian mafia. When, in reality, the *Bratva* had a very large price on his head. He was working in the states, selling guns to Lucky, but Gio was interfering in the deals.

"They think it's Dom; they've been questioning his old man's potential involvement." Carmine picked up a plastic uterus diagram.

"What do they have?" My heart started racing at the thought of Dom getting hurt.

"Speculation and not much else." He shrugged. "If these two families start feuding, you need to give up this fucking search and hightail it back to Cali. Lucky is already gunning for Gio. You don't need to be collateral damage." He held the diagram to my stomach, giving me a lascivious smile.

"Dom plans to send me into the Moretti compound," I said, staring at the ceiling. "I could get my answers."

"Be careful, Seph. If we're right about this, you're opening yourself up to a world you may not be able to escape."

My jaw clenched at the concern in his voice. "If we're right, these are the people who stole my identity in the first place. So, nothing matters besides taking him down." I closed the door behind me and started down the hallway. I just needed to confirm that Anthony Moretti was the ringleader I was chasing, then they could all kill each other for all I cared.

"You're already on the Agostinos' radar," Carmine said from the doorway, causing my steps to falter. "Apollo's been asking Sienna Agostino to get information on you."

Fuck. They could look, but they wouldn't find anything. I was a ghost. Adoption records, fingerprints, and police reports were deleted by the best of the best. That being said, my stomach was still unsettled the entire ride back to Dom's. I didn't want their attention.

"I take it everything went well?" Dom stood in the foyer as I entered the house.

The hair on the back of my neck rose from the tone of his voice. I tried locking down my exhausted expression as I dazzled him with a look full of lust.

Above all else, Dom Moretti was an attractive man: tall, broad-shouldered, with a ruggedly handsome face. He was dangerous... a *bad* man. Yet, like a moth to the flame, I allowed him to possess me in every way. No, not allowed. I wanted it. I wanted *him.*

Even now, I could feel his anger but found myself unable to escape as I strutted towards him. My hips swayed with their natural rhythm as my stiletto heels clicked across the marble foyer.

"Of course." I placed my hands against his chest and leaned up to kiss him.

I caught the look, but it was too late. His hand latched into my hair and tugged my head backwards, forcing my neck to tilt. His other hand held on to my throat with a tight and threatening grip, silence stretching between us as he stared down at me in annoyed dominance.

I racked my brain, trying to remember what I could've done to piss him off, but nothing came to mind. It wasn't because of my visit with Carmine—we would've seen it coming.

"Tell me, pet." His voice was deep and gravelly, sending a ripple of pleasure through me. "Why can't you seem to… fucking obey me? Hm?" I didn't have the slightest clue what he was talking about.

"I do my best to please you, sir." I cringed as he tugged me tighter.

"Do you, though?" The question dripped from his mouth, filled with so much animosity my heart felt like it would explode. I didn't answer, my anxiety heightening and forcing the words to die on my tongue. "I allow you to live here. I protect you." We started moving up the stairs, his grip unrelenting as I stumbled along with him. "I thought we were on the same page.

"Dom, please," I cried as I lost my footing, but his grip kept me in place.

"Do you think you're better than them? 'Cause I let you live in my house?" He opened the bedroom door and shoved me inside—the momentum made me stumble. "You're all the same, pet. I could send you back to them with a snap of my fingers." He demonstrated the gesture as he spoke. And when I didn't respond, he stormed forward—his long, angry strides pounding on the floor.

"Wh-what do you want, sir?" I asked, hanging my head in shame.

Suddenly, exhaustion swept over my entire body. My mind was playing tricks on me. I didn't know what was and wasn't real anymore. I wanted to be a different girl with a different life. I was so tired that I was falling victim to his stupid games. I hadn't *done* anything. He just wanted to exude his power over me—to dominate me.

I was tired of battling with myself, to be the strength and the face of this movement… of this war. I couldn't break… I couldn't allow anyone to break me, or evil would win.

You're too strong and have come too far to bow out now. Suck it up, bitch.

My hands slowly shifted to his belt and began to undo it, before pulling down his zipper. I watched his angry brown globes deflate; his erection pressed the limits of his slacks. I *needed* this more than he did right now. I wanted him to fall apart at my hands.

"That's a good girl." He stroked my hair as I slid him into my mouth, licking him from head to balls before taking him deep. I worked him up and down, listening to his groans of pleasure. He was long and thick, and my jaw ached from the pressure as I kept moving.

"Do you like that?" I asked, licking around his head before swallowing it deep again, over and over.

He didn't say anything—I didn't expect him to—just continued watching me with an undiluted expression of awe. I reached between my legs, and my hand slid under my skirt, finding myself wet and ready. This was us—a push and pull of demented affection.

And I hated how much I fucking *loved* it.

"That's right. You take it all, pet." He moaned the words. "Nothing's fucking sexier than my little pet on her knees, taking her punishment."

He jerked himself out of my mouth and pulled me to my feet, forcing me to lie down on the chaise lounge. He ripped my panties off and tugged my skirt to my hips in one practiced move. His hands dove between my thighs and his eyes burned bright with what he found.

"You're fucking soaked. Goddamn, Perse." He growled as he lifted my legs in the air and spread them wide; his cock hung heavy and ready at my entrance. "You do love what I do to you, pet. Now, I'm going to give you… every fucking *inch* of what you love." He thrusted forward and buried himself deep as I screamed.

Where Dom was normally controlled and precise, this time he fucked me with wanton abandonment. His movements were unrivaled and unrestrained, a combination I'd come to love. And loved to *come*.

His words and actions showed the true dominance that I needed. I could instantly feel my mind clearing. The stress and confusion were disappearing into a cloud of smoke as my orgasm approached.

His large palm wrapped around my throat and pulled me forward as he stared into my eyes. I gripped his wrist with both of my hands, hanging on to him as if he were my everything. With no preamble to the explosion, his feral gaze made me crash and burn in an unending orgasm.

White stars exploded from behind my eyelids; the sensations were overwhelming and invigorating in the same breath. The relentless pounding ceased as his expression softened, his movements slow and almost loving.

"I know you're fighting numerous battles, Perse. And not just in here." He tapped my head. "But during your pursuit of everyone in that vault… don't lose yourself."

"I'm not." I was breathless as dishonesty poured from my mouth.

"Lies." He slapped my thigh as if he could read my mind. And his pace quickened once again. "We've needed to cage your blackouts more frequently. You, my little pet, are falling apart at the seams. And at this rate… I don't know if we can keep putting you back together."

"I'll get my answers soon enough," I muttered, as another earth-shattering orgasm rose to the surface.

"I'll make sure you get your answers, Perse. But at what cost? What are you willing to sacrifice to end this?" His eyes were resolute. He was concerned… worried about the course I was choosing to run. At full speed ahead. Without looking back.

He finished, tucked himself into his pants, and left the room. I walked into the bathroom and stared at my reflection in the mirror. My pale skin was reddened by his five o'clock shadow, and my lips were bruised from his harsh kiss. My irises were blue and my pupils clear—a sight for sore eyes after the last few weeks of internal conflict seeping from my pores.

I could still feel the cavernous depths of his sincerity, his offer to help me, but in the end… only one of us would survive. I refused to cower and lose because of an irrational attachment to a man. To this man. Because men like Dominic Moretti were the exact type I sought to punish. Their ability to accumulate money, power, and dominance came with the misguided belief they were above retribution.

And I was going to show them just how wrong they were.

Chapter Seven
PERSEPHONE

"**A**re you sure this is a good idea?" I asked Dom as he connected my garter belt to my pantyhose. "And do the other maids really wear this?" I motioned to the skimpy ensemble.

"They don't. But when you fuck up, it'll temper my father's rage," Dom said, snapping me into my outfit.

"Just checking." My response was mumbled and pathetic.

This was so fucked... This entire plan had disaster written all over it, and yet, here we were. A slutty maid outfit wouldn't be enough to save me if his father caught me snooping around his house. I was aware this could very well lead me to my death.

The last few weeks had been nothing but dead ends and shoot-outs, mixed with a few other fits of mayhem. But... I still had nothing when it came to looking for Mr. Brown Eyes. The Agostinos were pretty much at war with the Russians, and Dom was salivating at the opportunity to punish his brother.

Dom had lost his father's trust years ago, when he tried to turn his back on the family business. He built a separate empire in spite of his forebearer. His power and tactics were insurmountable, compared to the rest of the family. Now, he had to get creative in order to learn what his father and brother had planned… i.e., he had to use me.

His precious sister was safe under the Agostinos' protection while war broke out. But as they hunkered down to defend one side, they didn't know their territory had been infiltrated—overrun with Californian *made men*.

Carmine had sent Matteo to the east coast in support, but it was all closing in around me. I didn't have my answers, yet the Ragetti heir was satisfied with torching the city without them. I should have just let him kill them all—God knew they deserved it.

But I couldn't let that happen, not until I knew for sure.

"Chin up. Eyes and ears open," John said from the foyer as we headed to the door.

Women were peculiar creatures. We had natural-born instincts to protect those we loved, willingly throwing ourselves into the burning ruin around us. We were strong. We were brave. But… me, well, I was stupid. No good would come from this. And I was certain all of us knew as much.

Dom drove to his parents' estate and the car ride was filled with strained silence, each lost in our own worlds. A small jealous part of me was filled with anxiety, over having to interact with his sister. And I hated that I allowed her to make me feel inferior. But she had two families swooning at her feet—valiant men, armed and ready to take on the world for her. I knew Dom cared for me in his own way, but it wasn't even close to the *bella sorrelina*: the beautiful little sister.

The Italian goddess on a pedestal that the Morettis—and now the Agostinos—stood beneath to watch and protect. She was engaged to the devil and his demons frolicked at his command. Dom didn't seem to care for anything other than her well-being. No matter how many times I told myself I could handle this, that I was strong enough, a large part of me hated the circle she had around her. She was their angel, the light to the darkness they shrouded themselves in. The girl never knew true pain or torment in her entire life. Everything had been handed to her on a fucking diamond-encrusted platter.

Dom gripped the steering wheel tighter as the metal gates opened, and he pulled us down the long driveway. The red-brick mansion slowly came into view. It was huge, far larger than necessary for a family of five. It showed just how much power Anthony Moretti thought he'd amassed.

Stepping in through the kitchen, he introduced me to an older woman by the name of Ethel, who would show me the ropes. My palms itched, and my clothing felt like it was strangling me. Ethel was in her sixties with a soft voice and kind eyes. She made it a point at almost every turn to warn me to "watch out" for *Mr. Moretti*, that he was "no good to young girls" like me. She wasn't helping my anxiety and my internal alarm bells screamed their reluctance.

I followed her around as she showed me where the mops and buckets were to scrub the floor. My outfit made her pause as she silently shook her head before telling me someone else would handle it. This was clearly not her first rodeo dealing with girls being hired for their looks and not their cleaning skills.

Then I met Serafina Moretti, Dom's mother. I wanted to hate her... really, really wanted to. But her beautiful face was kind and filled with a softness you'd assume wouldn't have survived being married to a man like Anthony. She was thin and had a natural seductive gait to her walk. She hugged me close and welcomed me to her home, asking me to be mindful of her antiques when dusting.

She didn't even blink at my ensemble or question my teetering heels. And it made me angry. No… it made me *fucking* furious. She was so used to her husband's antics with women in her own home that she didn't even flinch when whores were thrusted in her face. I felt the urge to yell and cry for her—to demand she want more for herself.

But I wouldn't.

When Ethel warned me of a particular hallway, her face told me all I needed to know. The fear that morphed her features meant there was a high probability that this was where I'd find my answers. I swallowed past the bile rising in my throat and cautiously headed to the closed door at the end of the corridor.

"You've got some balls on you, you little shit." A deep voice echoed from behind the wood paneling.

"You're giving the term *family business* a whole new meaning," another responded.

"Yeah, well, you pay your fucking dues to me as your father and the head of this family. I am going to get what's fucking owed to me, boy." It was Anthony Moretti.

"Like your fucking dues to the Agostinos? You might cower to them, but I sure as fuck won't," Gio growled back.

"Who the fuck do you think you're talking to? I am your father and what I say in this family—for this family—goes. Your little schemes against them will exterminate our entire line." Their voices were rising and echoing down the hall. "You have no idea what you're doing."

"They can't fucking touch me." Gio sounded louder, and I could tell they were walking towards the door.

"You're not untouchable. You're just fucking stupid! You think I want to fucking pay them? I don't! I'm protecting this family!" Anthony seemed tired and beaten down. *"Dammi la forza."*

"Fuck them." Even I could hear the younger Moretti's assurance through the door. *"È la mia città."*

"We cannot afford to take on the Agostinos *and* the Ragettis. And that's exactly what will happen if this isn't orchestrated the right way." Anthony's words had my heart lodged in my throat. "The Ragettis will destroy this entire family if Mario-Fucking-Agostino tells them the truth."

"I'll fucking handle it." Before I could order my body to move, the door flew open, and I stumbled back.

I looked up to see the offending individual glaring down at me with pure rage in his brown eyes. Eyes so similar… I hated that he shared them with Dom. Gio's eyes were cocky and demeaning, possessing a blank cruelty.

"What the fuck are you doing here?" Anthony shouted from behind his son. Shoving Gio out of the way, he grabbed my arm and pulled me into the office.

Gio followed us inside and slammed the door closed, the walls shaking with the enraged gesture. I was a lamb in the lion's den as the two men surrounded me. Anthony shoved me into the chair, his eyes immediately dropping south before looking up at me again with a new expression—one I didn't like.

"Eavesdropping?" Gio asked, arms folded across his chest.

For all that I had heard about him, he didn't seem to be foolhardy and unintimidating. The man before me was composed with a raging storm brewing beneath the surface. But the imminent downpour seemed… calculated. Who was this man?

"I-I-I was dusting, sir." My voice shook with actual fear. I didn't even have to pretend. I was petrified.

"This wing is off-limits!" Anthony leaned into my face. "Unless you were looking for something specific from me?" He placed a firm grip on my thigh, painful and unrelenting.

I looked to Gio for help, but his expression was indiscernible. I couldn't put my finger on it, but his eyes seemed distant and vacant… confused. They weren't hungry or angry, just blank with a hint of realization—all of which terrified me even more.

"You heard something." He stepped behind the chair, leaning over me. "What did you hear?"

"No-nothing, sir." I gulped down the acid building in my throat.

"Liar." Gio ripped me from the seat, a strong hand on my neck. My body screamed in agony as he lifted me in the air and slammed my back against the wall. "You… what's your name?" He growled —a low, menacing sound assaulting my ears just as much as if he had been screaming.

I was frozen in place, my mind scattered by all the ways I assumed they were going to kill me. This conversation told me all I needed to know—what Carmine wanted to know. Mario and Anthony were guilty; they'd offered lies to the Ragettis. It was all so clear now. This was the end of the line for me, and I still didn't have the answers to my own questions.

"Tell. Me. Your. Name." Gio's unparalleled aggression forced my body to shake.

Such a disappointment. The hooded man's whispered words

bounced around inside my skull as my lungs screamed and pleaded for air.

"No!" And then it happened.

Anthony and Gio were gone, leaving me with the hissed threat and those emblazoned brown eyes. The scars on my back from the whip burned alive, sending me spiraling into agony.

I could hear and feel the leather as it snapped to life and painfully shredded my flesh. Unwanted tears I hadn't spilt in years ran harrowing streaks down my cheeks as I begged and cried for mercy. I stared into his blank, soulless eyes that gave nothing away. And as much as I hated him—hated what was happening to me— his declaration that I was a disappointment was a red-hot poker to my soul.

It was all a fucking nightmare. None of it was real.

"Give me. Your fucking. Name." Gio grabbed my upper arms and hauled me to my feet.

The door to my vault rattled and groaned with the pressure being applied. The metaphorical steel could only be held together for so long before it would finally explode. The memories, the names, the faces—all of it was at my fingertips. Just one step and I could end it, tell the world my secrets.

"Gio. Enough," Anthony ordered, sounding bored as he walked around his desk. "Whatever she could've heard is useless." He waved me off with a dismissive flick of his hand.

Gio wasn't so sure, one heavy palm moving from my bicep to my throat. His silent stare down was spurring my subconscious demons to life. They started laughing and dancing inside my head. My neck twitched as I tried to maintain control, and he slammed me into the wall, the internal struggle replaced by a more tangible pain.

"Stop lying and tell me who you are." I was ready to bare my soul as the scars on my back seemed to phantasmically spill blood.

I blinked and pleaded for my mind to stop its games. Imploring my brain cells to process the physical scene before me. But they were gone, the reality of my situation superseded by my trauma.

"Bella is coming down for break—what the fuck is going on in here?" I could hear Dom's voice approach, but couldn't see past my memories.

"This little tart was eavesdropping in the hall." The Moretti patriarch once again waved off his concern before grabbing his cell phone. "I'll be down shortly. All of you need to leave." And just like that, we were dismissed.

I could finally inhale, snapping back to life. My limbs were cramped, my fingers frozen in place, and I couldn't bend them. My hands stalled in open palms, hanging uselessly at my sides—my fight exhausted.

Once in the hallway, Dom turned on his heel and slammed his brother against the wall. They grappled with each other for a few minutes—fist for fist—until Dom managed to lock Gio's arms down.

"The fuck is the matter with you? Turning into him now? Beating up on women?" Dom challenged his brother, the two men filling the small space of the hallway with their hatred for one another.

"Like you give a fuck about some little slut." Gio shoved Dom backwards, stepping around him as he charged for me. "I don't know why you're here, you little bitch. But I'm throwing you out on your ass before you get a chance to do anything."

"I-I…" I couldn't swallow down my fear, my regret.

The regret I felt for the little girl who was eaten up and spit back out: alive but tarnished. Far too young to have seen such brutality. I regretted allowing my need for vengeance to consume me. But most of all, I regretted who I'd become.

I was being used by Dom for his own agenda against his brother. He pretended to care about me and my mission, but it was always about what was in it *for him*. I was useful when it came to getting answers and warming his bed. Nothing more.

I would never be anything more.

"Enough, Gio. She's with me." His tone was of pride, of the ownership he held over me.

"With you." It wasn't a question as he stared me down before a knowing smirk lit up his face. He recognized me. "What a delicious little treat. I bet you like dancing on his stage and riding his *pole*." I didn't have time to respond before they started fighting again.

"Enough!" Anthony suddenly appeared from the threshold of his office, his phone pressed to his ear as he slammed the door closed. Again.

"Don't fucking touch her," Dom grunted, adjusting his suit jacket.

"And what is your little whore's name?" Gio questioned, but I still stayed silent.

"None. Of your. Fucking business." Dom grounded out each word.

"If I had her… I'd lock her up. In a vault." He threw the words over his shoulder as he disappeared down the hallway. His choice in vocabulary had my anxiety spiking even higher.

"Oh, please, dear. You must help serve breakfast. It's Miss Bella's birthday." Ethel came charging around the corner, snatching my hand as I followed after her in a daze. "You stupid girl. I warned you away from them! Now you have the attention of all three. Nothing good will come of that." I looked up into Ethel's concerned eyes. "I am going to talk to Mrs. Moretti. Today is your last day." Her words were soft, filled with worry rather than threat. I couldn't even be mad at her. It made me wonder how I would've turned out if I had a fierce protector like her growing up. She handed me a tray and ushered me towards the dining room.

"He just showed up unannounced and completely off-kilter? Something is going on." Dom's voice cemented my feet, and I was unable to move from the shadows.

"It seems Bella's engagement set him off. You know he hates Lucky and that family." Anthony dismissed his son's concerns like they were nothing.

"He's begging for his death, stealing from Lucky." Dom sounded almost worried about his brother.

"It appears your sister is valuable after all. Her hold on Lucky seems to be working in our favor. The Agostino guard dog paid Gio a *little* visit and assured us your brother wouldn't be attending tonight."

Fucking Bella, always the goddamn angel amongst demons.

I felt as though the girl could literally do no wrong. Straightening my spine, I went to serve breakfast to the celestial herself—with every intention of not shoving it down her throat.

A trip to hell was a guarantee after I forced her to choke on my sorrow.

Chapter Eight
PERSEPHONE

*S*etting up the breakfast buffet, I could feel Dom's gaze burning a hole in my back. I knew if I looked at him, I'd break down. My hands were already shaking, and my mind struggled to maintain its limited sanity. Instead, I opted to keep myself busy and piled food onto the plates.

Just as I was about to make my escape to the kitchen, I saw two figures enter the room. My blonde hair fell in front of my face as I got my first up-close and personal look at Mirabella Moretti. As much as I wanted to deny it, she was a gorgeous woman. Not much older than I was, and about my height and build. Her long black locks fell softly down her back, and even in workout clothing, she was stunning. She had a natural poise to her stride that only cultured rich girls could possess. Though I found hers to be inviting and pleasant, unlike the other silver-spooned bitches I'd encountered.

Anthony went into detail about the extravagant birthday the Agostinos were throwing for her. She smiled, and damn, if the bitch didn't look as sweet as everyone said she was.

My thoughts quickly shut off as her father turned towards me, barking orders to fetch the girl a plate. You know, since the princess couldn't be tasked with feeding herself—I wouldn't mind if she choked on it.

Unsure of how to proceed, I piled a dish full of buffet selections and placed it in front of her, doing my best to ignore her gracious expression. I almost smiled back but thankfully her father chose that moment to freak out.

"The fuck is wrong with you? Stupid, stupid girl! She has a party tonight! She gets what her mother has!" Lunging for the plate before I could take it, he flipped it off the table. The appetizing waffles, which were piled high with whipped cream and strawberries, plastered the front of my uniform. I shook in fright, waiting for the commotion to ensue. "Jesus Christ! Incompetence. The fuck were you thinking, Dominic?" He snarled before exiting the room, rambling down the hallway, as I dropped to my knees to retrieve the plates.

Bella and her mother kneeled beside me, cleaning up the mess from the floor and whispering apologies. My limbs felt like dead weight and my mind was in a tailspin. I was petrified that my monsters were going to let loose at any moment and ruin my plans. In that same breath, I was disheartened by my own weakness in allowing these men to treat me like this.

"What did he mean, Dominic?" Bella asked her brother in a small, innocent voice.

He seemed lost to the plethora of unspoken punishments sure to come my way. I was both pleased and terrified; my breaths came out as harsh pants as I tamped down my inner demons. But it was like sand pouring through my hands… a losing battle.

Such a disappointment. The voice once again bounced around in the confines of my mind, and I had to bite my cheek to hold in my gasp—a fearful squeak slipping free. I could sense a breakdown was on its way. I grabbed the plate from the floor and ran from the dining area. Discarding the empty dish in the sink, I locked myself in the back bathroom. I stared at the girl in the mirror, dumbfounded by the frailty I saw in front of me.

"Get your shit together," I muttered to the blue eyes glaring back at me while swiping at the smeared mascara.

"There is too much shit going on for him to ruin this," Anthony said from outside the bathroom door.

"It's too late now. I'll destroy him if he gets in my way," Gio responded as their voices shuffled and moved down the hall. Their conversation continued, but it faded along with their footsteps.

I couldn't let these men hurt him.

"Without sacrifice, there is no great reward. So, fuck them... The elite use the weak to make those sacrifices and take the reward."

My breath caught in my throat, and my mouth went dry. *Those words.* They've haunted my memories since my abduction. *Anthony-fucking-Moretti.* I knew it. I knew it was one of them, and they just confirmed my hunch with one simple statement of pure callous ingenuity. When he had me pinned in that chair in his office, I didn't notice it in his eyes, but it was him—those words proved it.

I held my breath as my mind raced with indecision. The strong part of me wanted to rip the door open and attack, show them I was no longer their prey. The other, more reasonable part of me knew I was too damaged and unprepared. Indecision rattled my nerves as I felt my body shake and my lucidity wane.

"No," I muttered as I continued to stare at myself in the mirror. My makeup was running down my face and my eyes were wild, unfocused. Errant thoughts plagued my mind as I considered the prospect of Dom being involved. It was no secret he had his hand in several pots, but could he be a part of... this?

It was his fucking father...

I needed to get the fuck out of this house. Sweet Serafina was turning a blind eye to her husband's business. Precious Bella wouldn't save me or ask her new fiancé to help. And with Dom... I didn't know what was and wasn't real.

He locked me in my cage to secure me, to save me from myself, empowering me to charge forward. But by that same token, he was the restricting grip around my chest. He could easily crush my ribs and cause the splintered bone to pierce my heart. I belonged to him... completely. But he was the furthest thing from *belonging to me.* And at that moment, I realized I had only one form of recourse.

He answered on the second ring. "Carmine, please." I hated myself for the emotional plea. "I need you to come get me from the Morettis."

"Is she okay?" Matteo shouted in the background.

"Fifteen minutes," he clipped and hung up. I waited ten before stepping into the kitchen. I was alone and didn't hesitate to kick off my heels. Tiptoeing towards the back door, I was about to open it when I heard Dom talking to his sister in the hall. Every part of me screamed to run outside, but I couldn't move.

"Go now." I jumped at Ethel's voice. "Never, never come back." She gave me a sad smile and patted my shoulder in reassurance, as she all-but-pushed me over the threshold.

I hid behind ugly green shrubbery until my phone lit up with a text message. Clicking the location, I ran towards the dot on the screen, charging as fast as I could to get to the idling car. The door was barely open as I threw myself inside, and Carmine pulled away before it closed.

"Seph… breathe, girl. I need you to breathe and get your shit straight," he ordered, though his eyes never left the road.

"It's all falling down around me." I gasped, trying to calm my racing heart while begging my mind to do the same.

"Stay with me, Seph. Imma need answers, babe." He kept his tone calm and loud, but he was fading into the background. A burst of giggles consumed me and I started clapping my hands, as my faculties regressed to my happy place. "Fucking hell, Seph" he shouted. But the sound fell on deaf ears as that ever-so-sweet nothing drove me down to my familiar pit of despair.

I thrived in the darkness, alone. It was my safe place but even better… it was my nirvana. It was where my dreams became everyone else's nightmares.

Chapter Nine
CARMINE RAGETTI

"Goddamn it." I growled, carrying an unconscious Persephone into the warehouse.

"What happened?" Matteo came storming down the staircase towards us.

"The fucking Morettis, that's what happened." I placed Persephone on the bed.

"I fucking warned you about this. She can't handle this on her own, and now she's fucking the enemy! Damn it, Carmine!" Matteo crossed his arms over his chest.

Stepping out of the room, I closed the door behind us as we approached our makeshift bar. This warehouse was one of my first large purchases as a teenager, when I started plotting. It's buried under hidden names but central enough in New York that I could watch my enemies anonymously. And the fucking Agostinos and Morettis were public enemy number one and two. And I was here to make sure they paid. In blood.

I always knew this day would come. That these two families would have to be dealt with, and I was just the man to do it. My father turned a blind eye to the east coast, focusing on the west and allowing our rivals to assume we were stupid.

But I wasn't my father's son. No, I was a fucking god among men and anyone looking to take me on… they'd be struck down. One way or the other.

"This is her mission. Who the fuck are we to tell her to back off?" I questioned, furious with his disrespect. "I fucking told you not to hire her that day she came clicking her clear heels on our doorstep. You didn't fucking listen *then,* so why should I listen *now?*"

"You're really comparing giving a homeless girl a job to sending her to her death…" He stopped short, sighing, before he turned on his heel and went to the bar. I wanted to laugh at him as I remembered the first time I laid eyes on the crazy blonde with the dead stare.

"Auditions are Tuesday nights, from six to twelve," I said, not looking up from my paperwork.

"They told me at the door, but I need money now." The plea was scratchy, broken.

"Not my problem." I refused to acknowledge what was probably another junkie.

"A girl dying on your front steps would be a problem." She had a little fire to her voice, making me snort. If only she knew who she was talking to, then she'd shut the fuck up and leave my office.

"That's why I have a dumpster, sweetheart." I flipped through another report, going over the club's inventory.

"That crooked-toothed motherfucker is back again." Matteo barged into the room, making the chick squeal. "A present? For me? Oh, brother, you shouldn't have."

I sat back with a smirk, finally looking up at the girl. Matteo was circling her like a vulture—practically touching her, he was so close. He loved to make people uncomfortable, almost as much as I did. Except, the moment this little bird's eyes fluttered in his direction, he stopped.

God. Damn. Him. Matteo was cold, defiant, and had an innate ability—like all the men in our family—to make your skin burn as we flayed it open with our eyes. You'd sweat and moan as we ripped you to shreds without even touching you. But wounded animals were a soft spot for my brother.

"Please. Look, I know auditions aren't until next week, but I just got into

town and need cash. I'm good at dancing; just give me a chance. I need the tips to find a room and food." She turned her pleas to him this time.

Her eyes were the color of the bluest serene ocean you'd ever seen. But there was a ripple beneath them that warned of a tsunami preparing to unleash destruction. He wasn't going to throw her out, not a chance in hell. He was fucking crazy, a master when it came to debauchery, but he had a thing for wounded birds.

"You've danced before?" he asked, crossing his arms over his chest.

"Not by choice," she whispered towards the ground.

Matteo snapped his neck in my direction, concern consuming his thought process. I rolled my eyes; he was going to keep her for himself. The more broken, battered, and beaten down, the more likely he was to trip over his own feet trying to save them.

"We don't take in strays."

Her head twisted towards me and anger morphed her angelic features. "I'm not a fucking stray. I earn top-fucking-dollar and I don't take pity. Let me on the damn stage, and I'll show you why you need to hire me." She dropped her bag onto the floor, her thin frame shaking with rage.

"It's Wednesday—it's dead out there," Matteo muttered, smirking at my agitated expression. "Crooked Teeth is here; he'll give us the honest truth." He laughed at my scowl, with the mere mention of the dead-beat motherfucker who still owed us money.

"We have a reputation for high-class, sweetheart." I went to continue but stopped as she started taking her clothes off.

"Fuck." Matteo coughed behind his hand, trying to cover a smile.

She was thin, but her body was proportionate, smaller perky breasts and a toned stomach. Her ass was fuller than you'd expect, and she had a natural seduction to her walk. She was in a plain black bra and thong. Kicking off her worn sneakers, she pulled scuffed heels from her bag before stepping into them. Then she spun without a word and stormed down the stairs and into the club.

"Let the street rat up." Matteo was already on the phone with the DJ. "What? She's fucking hot and needs a leg up in life. Why not let her lift that leg over my shoulder?" His look was filled with filthy promises, but he wasn't fooling anyone.

Those damaged blue eyes were going to haunt him if he didn't help her. She had the same debilitated expression our little sister wore after her... situation.

He couldn't protect Eva from the bad shit in our world, so this stray would make him feel better.

Buckcherry's "Crazy Bitch" started playing as she ascended the stage. The moment she climbed the pole, the entire room seemed to fall into silence. She crawled to the top with ease, swinging upside down, and held onto the cool metal with her thighs.

She was flawless and had the entire room entranced, a real moneymaker. But that wasn't worth the trouble I could tell she would bring to our door. We were already elbow deep in bullshit, due to our crazy-fucking-father starting a deadly shoot-out live on the news for all to see. Whatever she had going on wasn't worth the added headache.

"The girl has moves." Matteo stood at the window beside me as we watched her gyrate across the stage.

"The girl is going to be a problem. The answer is no." I turned back towards my seat as the song ended. And two minutes later, she stormed into the room. "You're…"

"Hired." Matteo grabbed her bag and ushered her out the door.

"Motherfucker." I threw a glass against the wall, cursing in agitation.

Ever since I started preparing to take over California, in my father's stead, I knew New York was going to be a problem. I knew Mario Agostino was to blame for my uncle's death. He may not have killed him, but Uncle Sal died in *his* city. No one fucked with my family and was lucky enough to keep breathing.

My father was certifiable, and an obstacle I was going to have to deal with sooner rather than later. In the meantime, Persephone was on a mission that would give both of us the answers we had been searching for. She'd get her peace… and I'd get their blood.

For years after my uncle's death, my family concentrated on owning California. Our power had transitioned to the east coast, merely out of fear of my father's impracticalities. He was known for being unhinged and creating carnage—no one wanted to deal with that. Mario respectfully stood down when we came for business.

"Brother, this fucking mission of yours is ridiculous anymore. You're so focused on revenge you're not seeing clearly." Matteo made me want to punch him in the goddamn face.

Breathing heavily, I turned towards the window and watched the sun slowly start to set. "It's them, Matteo. Both families are involved —I feel it. They're going to pay."

"And what of Eva?" It was subtle, but he braced himself, knowing the mere mention of my little sister incited violence.

"Leave her out of this." My knuckles cracked as I fought to stop myself from killing my own brother.

"What about her revenge?" His glass dropped as I turned on my heel and shoved him into the wall. "Tell me, brother, when does Eva get her peace?"

"Shut the fuck up!" I roared in his face, but he didn't falter. Pure hatred morphed his expression.

"It's your time to step up, to make right all the wrongs our father has done. To us. To our city." When I didn't speak, he continued, "To Eva. Goddamn it, Carmine. He should be your focus, not New York. Uncle Sal is dead and will stay dead. You're the one who can fix our family—what will it take to make you see that?"

"Pops is on borrowed time. I need to handle this first, to make sure that when I take over... nothing will be in my fucking way," I grunted. "Then we will go back to Cali and handle *him.*"

"We need to take Persephone and go now. Go before it is too late and we lose her. Eva's gone into hiding and Mom is a nervous wreck." I slammed him into the wall, spitting in his face, but he didn't relent. "And if you honestly think you will fuck with the Agostinos and come out unscathed, you're a fucking idiot."

"Eva will be fine; this won't last much longer. We'd be back on the west coast if it wasn't for the promise I made *you,* remember? No war without confirmation. Well, that mess..." I pointed at the thin wall separating us from Persephone. "...is definitely our fucking confirmation. Once I get it, nothing will hold me back from an all-out war and making Mario Agostino suffer."

The plan was forming in my head. I had already done the groundwork. I knew exactly how I was going to ensure I came out on top. The Morettis were damned—come hell or highwater, I'd kill them. But killing the Agostinos was a riskier game to play. I had to destroy them from the inside out; then I'd take something very near and dear to them.

"Don't… you can't be thinking of an innocent paying the price." He stopped. "Christ, you are. What if it was Eva?" His head was reeling, and I knew he wouldn't be aligned with my plan. And that's exactly why I didn't tell him. I was taking over as the head of our family, so my word was bond. I would execute this plan perfectly, cementing my bicoastal power.

"Shut the fuck up. They're all Agostinos; they're not innocent." I stepped back, trying to stop myself from destroying the room. "And we protect what is ours—they don't give *theirs* the same courtesy."

My body charged with excitement as my mind vividly replayed the plan I had been conjuring up. Since Matteo and I came into the city, we'd been scouring for answers and watching both families. I knew in my bones I was right, and Persephone's call told me as much.

I just needed her verbal confirmation, and then the metaphorical gloves were off. I knew exactly how to dismantle their entire organization. There was one move I could make that would ensure they fell, and I couldn't fucking wait to watch them crumble.

Persephone was pretending that she wasn't in love with Dom, which was a lie. But he was an even bigger idiot because he was falling for her too. That was a bomb just waiting to detonate: the fuse had already been lit, and the explosion was on the horizon.

I had them right where I wanted them. Once she told me the truth, I would set everything into motion and take my prize back to California with me. Ever since I was little, I never had much interest in toys. That was until now. This plaything was mine, and I wouldn't let anyone else have it.

The Agostinos believed they were only as strong as their weakest family member—or so they liked to remind everyone. I had plans to show them they were all wrong, that they were weak *because* of that misguided belief. They had no clue what was awaiting them.

I could taste my revenge. It was metallic in flavor and not much different from blood. It was sweet, like a fine wine I couldn't wait to savor. And I would thoroughly enjoy the sampling process.

Chapter Ten
PERSEPHONE

"Welcome back, did you have a nice trip?" Carmine's clipped tone stirred me awake. His face was a mixture of concern and annoyance, making me smile.

"How long have I been out?" I aggressively shook my head to clear the fog holding my brain prisoner.

"Shy of a day." His answer explained why he was annoyed—more than normal, that is.

"Fuck." I rubbed the heel of my hand against my eyes. "You were right. Dom is involved."

"Christ," he muttered, expelling a deep breath.

"Anthony Moretti. It's him, the ringleader. He… he talked about the elite. It… it's Dom's dad." I wiped at the snot that was pouring from my nose.

"Perse, you always suspected that. This entire time we knew there was a chance he was lying about his father's involvement." His nonchalance pissed me off.

"I know there was always a chance, and it didn't bother me before. Not until I realized that I…" I froze, not daring to go on.

"If you can't even say it aloud, then it's a lie. Because you *don't* love him." He waited a beat before continuing, "Doesn't necessarily mean Dom is involved."

"But a *chance* wasn't a *fact* before. There is really no way he couldn't know, right? Dom had to have some sort of idea?"

He shrugged at my questions. "Now you know. So… pull up those lacy little panties and do something about it." He was growing more impatient. His voice was harsh and held no room for argument, as if it was so simple.

The conflicting voices inside my head were screaming so loudly over top of each other that I couldn't think. I was drained, beaten, and utterly exhausted. I'd spent my entire life fighting so many fucking battles and it never ended—no matter how desperately I wanted it to.

"Tell me everything," he demanded, handing me two pills and a glass of water. Once I tossed them back, I spilled the details. I practically vomited all my sad truths: the game I thought I was controlling, it had beaten me.

That I'd been hunting Dom's father…

That everything I thought I knew… was fake…

That everything I thought I felt… was a *fucking* lie…

"I'm done. I can't do this anymore. At one point, I was okay if I died doing this. Because, for all the bad shit, I was doing twice as much good. Not anymore." I sighed. "You were right."

"I always am, but what are you talking about." Carmine looked triumphant.

"Anthony… he talked about the Agostinos destroying him because… of a secret Mario knows. About your family."

He stormed to his feet, grabbing a chair and throwing it against the wall. His roar of anguish accompanied the sound of the wood splintering and caused the floorboards to shake. "Dead! They're all fucking dead!" he bellowed.

He continued raging around the room, shattering anything within reach. When there was nothing left to grab, he started punching holes in the drywall with his massive fists. The tears came faster and I didn't bother wiping them away.

"I'm sorry," I muttered, as if I had anything to do with the whole fucked-up situation.

"Okay." He stopped and took a deep breath. "We've got answers, and now we act."

It was no secret that Carmine was here to murder and maim in the name of his family. Fuck, that didn't even come close to describing the pure malicious intent harbored inside his soul. He'd been on this hunt for most of his life. And now he had the answers he wanted. Like me, he was a slave to his given path. There wasn't anything we could do about it, other than hope we didn't lose ourselves in the process.

"I have an idea." He leaned back over the bed with a pensive look. "You're not done with the Morettis."

"You can't expect me to go back there. Carmine, I can't." My chin wobbled, and my heart raced as fear settled in my bones.

"I'm sorry, Seph. But this is far from over." I hated his smirk *and* the fact that his words straightened my spine.

"I don't know if I'm strong enough," I whispered, despising how weak I sounded. "How am I supposed to…?"

"Because you're a fucking survivor. This was all you, babe, no one else. From day one, you were at the helm, guiding this all to fruition. You started this, and now it's time to end it." He squeezed my shoulder.

"Okay," I conceded, pulling myself to the end of the bed.

"Okay?" His scowl morphed into a satanic smirk that made me smile. "Okay! I want to incite chaos from within their families!" he shouted, tugging me to my feet!

"Yes." Even I could hear the lack of confidence in my own voice. "Where do we start?" I was exhausted, but the finish line was in sight.

"You've already started, sweetness," he admonished as he tucked a stray piece of hair behind my ear. "We keep up what we've got in place to take them down. Once and for all."

"Dom's sister… Bella. They're throwing a party for her. All the Agostinos and Morettis will be in the same room, at the same time." My heart ached as I said the words and pictured Dom.

"You sure, Seph? You know I won't be able to just stroll inside." He motioned with his hand, sweeping down his large body. "But I need your ears open and head in the game to make sure everything goes off without a hitch."

"I'll have to do some groveling, but Dom hasn't turned me down… yet." I laughed humorlessly, thinking about our *relationship*.

We were like two hurricanes just off the coast—an incredible, breathtaking sight to behold. *From afar.* But up close, we were nothing but turbulent winds and promised ruin—clashing to bring about total destruction.

"I will do this. No matter the cost," I mumbled to myself as we approached Dom's neighborhood.

"There's my crazy bitch." He chuckled as he pulled the car over. "Show those teeth, and go get 'em, tiger."

I skipped down the driveway, forcing a smile on my face. We were almost home free. A decade of hunting, and it was finally time to tear into the meat. To enjoy a taste.

"I'm home!" I sang into the security box next to the iron gate.

Chapter Eleven
PERSEPHONE

"*W*ell, aren't you a sight for sore eyes?" Norm gave me an amused expression as he leaned against the limo. I didn't answer, merely wiggled my fingers in an exaggerated wave and kept twirling in circles towards the door.

I pretended not to notice the tremble of my hands or the slight shake in my legs as I climbed the front steps. I was stunned by indecision over whether or not I should ring the bell. Thankfully, John opened it before I had to decide.

"You're just a twisted little wet dream, aren't you?" He motioned towards my outfit, forcing me to look down.

I was a fucking mess. Inside and out. My stockings were torn, and only one of my heels was latched around the ankle. The ruffled skirt of the maid outfit was matted and misshapen, so it gave a flash of my panties. I could feel my long blonde tresses were a tangled mess and could only imagine what my face looked like. I was the epitome of the *walk of shame* right now.

"You know he doesn't like his toys played with," I said as I tried to swallow my nerves.

"You may *toy* with others, but we all know you belong to no one." He looked towards the stairs. "Better watch yourself, Persephone. He isn't pleased." I could feel his concern, but he made no attempt to stop me.

"I know how to make it all better," I muttered as I walked around him and entered the house. I took my shoes off, wandered to Dom's office, and knocked on the door.

"Yeah." His calm voice filtered from behind the wood paneling. *Too calm.*

I opened the door before quickly slipping inside and leaning against it. "Did you miss me, baby?" I purred, flicking my hair off my shoulder and strutting to his desk on my tippy-toes.

"You're alive." His brown eyes assessed me, giving nothing away. "You see, I assumed you must be dead. Surely you wouldn't do something stupid like run from me. Am I right, pet?"

"I didn't know what else to do." Honesty was the best policy in order to avoid getting caught in a lie. "Your father and brother cornered me—it was too much."

"So, you tucked your tail between those sexy legs and ran. To where, exactly?"

Lie. Lie. Lie. And so I did. I lied my ass off. Like my life depended on it. And let's face it: my life more than depended on it. There were holes in my story, but his eyes didn't show if he planned to poke through them or not. He had to know, since nothing about me ever got past him. The man was like a drooling dog, and I was the juicy bone. His meaty fist latched on to my neck and tugged me closer.

"Did someone touch what was mine?" He wedged his nose under my ear and inhaled.

Black spots started dancing behind my eyes as he tightened his grip. And my core convulsed, as I felt the loss of consciousness slowly creeping in. He released his hold the moment I was about to go under, and my body crashed into his. My soul was tormented as I gasped for oxygen, trying to slow my erratic heart.

He held my hips as I continued to struggle to keep myself upright—greedily gulping in copious amounts of air. I dropped my forehead to his chest and internally scolded myself as his shirt absorbed the silent tears racking my body. I hated how weak he made me feel in one moment, then empowered the next.

"I thought they did something to you," he whispered against my temple, hugging me to him and stroking my hair. "I destroyed the fucking house trying to find you."

"I'm here," I muttered, tears tipping over the edge and pouring down my face—a tender finger stroked them away. "I'm sorry." The words were barely out of my mouth before his lips slammed on mine. A clash of skin, teeth, and moans swirled around us as we got lost in each other.

This was us. Fire and ice. Calamity and sexuality. Vodka and club soda. Not everyone understood it, but we mixed in our own way. His hands traveled down my body, feeling and groping his way around, as if our night apart had him forgetting me.

"You make me crazy," he murmured, his teeth grazing along my chin, my ear, and my neck. "But you need to be punished, pet."

"Yes, sir." I choked on a moan as he sucked my earlobe into his mouth, causing my skin to break out in goosebumps.

"That's just what I want to hear. Now, get on your knees and show me how sorry you are." His crude command only made me more eager to comply.

I stared up at him—my attention never wavering—as I dropped in front of him. Slowly and precisely, I unclasped his black leather belt and popped the button on his slacks. He wasn't wearing a jacket or tie, the top of his shirt open just enough I could see a glimmer of his strong chest.

And, fuck me, was it hot.

I reached inside the zipper and pulled his heavy length from the tight confines. His muscular thighs flexed and moved as I worked my hand up and down, enjoying his faltered breath. One pump, then two, before I latched my lips around the head, savoring his flavor. It was like a drug to me—a taste I couldn't even begin to describe. Powerful enough to put me six feet under. And heady enough to leave me content with that outcome.

I worked faster and faster, enjoying the sting when his hands clasped my hair and commanded my movements. The grip at the nape of my neck was painful but set a new rush of heat throughout my body, while the look of desire in his eyes threatened to burn me from the inside out. My own hands roamed down my midsection, attempting to stave some of the pleasure I was practically begging for.

"Ah-ah-ah." He twisted my hair tighter and paused, his cock still buried in my throat. "This isn't about you." He pivoted his hips and ground himself deeper inside me. He took a small step backwards, but his grip remained strong, forcing me to scramble in order to follow his movements.

My thighs shook as I balanced on my toes, squatting as I braced for his assault. His taste, the sensations, and the desire in his eyes were almost enough to make me combust without even touching myself. A few more strokes, and I felt him harden—his breathing ragged—before he erupted down my esophagus. In one swooping motion, he rotated me in his grip and forced me to bend over his desk. I was already prepared before the sting assailed my rear.

Smack. Smack. Smack.

He shredded my thin panties in one tug and rammed himself home, pounding deep and powerful inside me. With no chance to adjust to his size, he started a crazed rhythm of soft and tempestuous strokes that quickly took me to the edge of bliss. And just as I was about to leap over into paradise, he stopped, giving a few more whacks before he moved again.

"Fuck!" I screamed and choked as I came, barely registering his weight on my back as he followed.

"Jesus Christ, pet." He pulled himself out of me and threw my limp, naked body into his desk chair.

And just like that… I was back and in control.

He tucked himself into his pants before leaning against the edge of his desk. His eyes roamed my naked body—a mixture of eagerness and fascination—as if he wanted another round but was stuck in an internal debate.

I was insatiable and needed more from him. Opening my legs, I placed them over the sides of the chair and sank back into the upholstery, giving him a chance to see what he could have… if he'd just let go.

"Enough." With a rough grip on my knees, he slammed my legs shut. "Tell me. Everything," he ordered.

So, I did. *Minus a few key details.*

"They said the Ragettis?" he asked, scratching his head.

I nodded. "Yes. The Agostinos know something about it," I admitted, curious as to why the perplexed look on his face.

"My father killed a Ragetti to steal my mother from him. No one knew—we've kept it hidden for years. Mario must've found out somehow, and now he's holding it over my father's head."

Well, shit.

Oh, fuck… Carmine was going to be out for blood, and I had no clue as to how to protect Dom. Once I told him that the entire family knew, he'd destroy them all without hesitation.

"Where do we start?" I asked, watching him tap his finger to his upper lip.

But if I learned Dom knew of his father's role in my downfall, no matter how much I thought I loved him, I'd kill Dom myself. No one was safe, when it came to me getting what I was owed. And I was owed blood—an eye for a fucking eye.

Mirabella Moretti's joint birthday and engagement party was held in the ballroom of a lavish hotel in the center of the city, where all the Agostino children occupied apartment units. So, of course, this was an easy choice for the decadent affair. The theme was black, red, and expensive. The staff and I were dressed in black suits and dresses, only the blushing bride-to-be was allowed to wear white. *The center of attention.*

"Keep your head in the game," I growled at myself as I got busy pretending to do work around the room.

It was slowly filling up with guests in lavish gowns—weighed down by ostentatious jewelry. So much power and money in one small space, and yet they were oblivious to the *real* luxuries they possessed. Most of them wouldn't know pain and suffering if they tripped over a starving child. So self-absorbed with their own mediocrity, and putting on a show, they turned a blind eye to the monstrosities surrounding them.

I stepped to the edge of the bar and slowly worked on opening the bottle of wine in my hand as I listened to Apollo, Lucky, and Mario converse amongst themselves.

"What do you know of Dominic Moretti's import business?" Lucky asked, just as the cork popped free.

I froze, as if they had any idea who the fuck I was. An ant under their shoe, in the grand scheme of things, ensured I wouldn't be on their radar… unless I garnered Apollo's attention.

"Besides it being lucrative enough to be our largest paycheck on the docks, nothing. Why?" Mario Agostino, the head of the family, announced.

Disgusting.

"How about the fact that the income he is paying us is the proceeds from selling women?"

The eldest Agostino scoffed at the question, realizing much too late no one else was laughing. "You're serious?" he asked.

Lucky nodded. "One of my men informed me."

"Jesus Christ." Scanning the room, neither of them seemed to find what they were looking for. "Gio isn't coming, but Dominic is supposed to be here."

Their attentions were suddenly drawn to the staircase, and more specifically, the girl standing mid-descent. She was dressed in a white strapless gown which all-too-eagerly hugged her slight curves. Her neck bore the weight of an emerald and diamond necklace, the value of which could no doubt feed a small country.

Fucking spoiled.

Dom sat at the table near his father, his eyes glued to anyone and anything but me. The Agostino siblings surrounded Bella—each wearing masks of perfected beauty and poise in an attempt to hide their rotten souls. Their blood had been tainted from the moment of conception by the same man who would bring about their downfalls.

I had been around Anthony Moretti for a while now, and I couldn't place why I felt so calm. My head was focused, and I was determined to finish this. Tonight. Yet, where I'd assumed I'd cower near the man who haunted my dreams; instead, I felt… nothing.

A loud shrill laugh erupted, and I watched as the birthday girl went rigid. I looked towards the sound's origin, and a part of me wanted to bend over and howl in amusement at the newcomer's simple act of cruelty and defiance. Her designer dress was tight and… *white.* The girl wore the color, despite the explicit instructions forbidding it.

She was ballsy. I'd give her that.

Lucky and his men stormed over to their patriarch and whispered to each other in harsh tones. Apollo caught my attention as I stared at him from a safe distance. Even this far away, I could see his eyes were alight with mischief and terrible promises, which spurred me closer just to see the twinkle of carnage.

I watched as the Agostinos sped into motion, Lucky ordering his men about as they approached the girl and her date.

I grabbed another bottle of wine and went to make my rounds at his table. The hair on the back of my neck rose, and I glanced at Anthony Moretti. It wasn't him. I'd been subjected to his presence for hours now, without a tremor of hesitation.

Turning my head, I saw Gio stumbling through the crowd, and my breath stalled in my chest. My shaky hands splashed wine on Bella, and her brother was coming in hot. Pissed.

Oh, fuck.

Chapter Twelve
PERSEPHONE

*B*ella gasped the moment the wine hit her delicate hand, and I was about to apologize, but stopped when we made eye contact. She knew who I was—the whore in the maid's outfit—as she stared back at me with overtly suspicious, mismatched eyes. One green and one blue, each seeming to have their own swirl of recognition and wariness.

I stood tall and turned to leave the table but halted, caught by the curious and penetrating gaze of Sienna Agostino. She was tall, with dark chestnut hair styled in perfect curls down her back, her lithe frame wrapped in a designer gown. She blocked my way as her infamous Agostino steel-blue eyes assessed me with pure hatred.

The death glare momentarily confused me, until it all fell into place. Her beloved Apollo was chasing me… a ghost. He wanted answers, and she hated that she couldn't get any. She could practically smell the deception—taunting and beautiful—as it emanated from my pores. And it enraged her. I opened my mouth to tell her to *kindly fuck off* when Dom latched on to my arm, savagely tugging me away.

I couldn't suppress the whine that left me as his fingers dug into my skin. Bella darted towards her brother and started shouting accusations—demanding that he release me. His face glowed red with agitation. And the moment he let me go, I high-tailed it from the dining area.

I ran for the staff bathroom that was off to the side of the kitchen. The lights were dim, and it smelled like apples and cinnamon. I turned on the faucet and quickly dipped my hands under the cool water, splashing my face. As the silence descended over me, I breathed deeply to calm my racing heart. Just as I was about to make my exit, the door opened, and I faltered in my steps.

"I never would've believed it if I hadn't seen it for myself. A ghost, right before my eyes." Sienna Agostino crossed her arms over her chest and leaned her back against the closed door.

"I'm sorry?" I asked, confused as she cornered me.

"No one, and I mean no one, can escape my investigations. So, clearly, you must be a ghost to not show up on any system. Which means... you're up to something." She placed her wine glass on the counter and stepped closer to me. "When Apollo asked me to research some pretty... little doll on Dominic Moretti's arm, I didn't expect to find... well, nothing. So, tell me, little doll... what're you hiding, exactly?"

She was jealous, and it made me smile. On the inside anyway.

She was taller than me by several inches, and her fancy designer-label shoes only heightened the difference. She knew how to fight—or so the rumors went—while her visible muscle mass leaned towards those rumors being true. Anyone else would have been intimidated, but I'd seen bitches like her circling their prey. And when it came down to eat or be eaten... well, I had sharper teeth.

"I need to get back to work." I invaded her personal space, all but declaring I wasn't afraid.

"Why is Dominic Moretti's little plaything working at his sister's birthday party?" she asked with a snarl. "I guess he loves playing in the gutter and fucking the help."

I smirked. She was the epitome of a stereotypical *mean girl,* and she was challenging the wrong one. I'd seen the worst that there was in this world—and I'd survived it. She was New York's posh princess, pampered from the time she was in diapers. But under all that beauty and perfection was an insecure little girl, pining for a man who would *never* return her feelings.

"What is your problem, exactly? Is it my mere presence here? Or is it that *the help* is competition?" I stepped closer and looked up at her.

"What the hell are you going on about?" she growled, her hands on her hips.

"He had you research me because I am the mystery he wants in his bed. Our encounters are filled with sexual tension and the promise that he could, would, and will fuck me dirty." I watched, enjoying the view as her eyes filled with a mixture of sadness and rage.

"Watch your fucking mouth." Her words were quiet—though clearly venomous.

"Maybe later you can watch it for me. As I swallow his cock… whole." I smacked my lips together and winked, before stepping around her and exiting through the door.

I hated mean girls. *With a passion.* I'd spent my entire life plagued by turmoil, in the hopes of saving strangers from people like her, her family, and those they employ. Yet, she was crying over her unrequited love for a man who couldn't even comprehend the definition.

I'd seen it in his eyes, his actions, and the stories I'd heard about the devil's right-hand man. He may have *cared* for her out of a sense of loyalty, but a psychopath like Apollo Deluca was incapable of more.

I smiled to myself as I skipped down the darkened hallway towards the kitchen. But for the second time this evening, the hair on the back of my neck raised, stalling my steps and forcing me to scan my surroundings. Earlier, the confined space had been bright and busy; now, it was empty and half of the bulbs were out. My heart pounded in my rib cage, and my breathing suspended in fright —virtually suffocating me.

I ducked into the kitchen in an obscured corner to try to get myself under control. Sienna walked down the hallway a second later, her heels clanking on the concrete flooring. I heard a gasp as she disappeared from my line of sight, and my heart threatened to explode in my chest—the fear forcing me to stay put.

After some time, I swallowed down that too-familiar sense of foreboding and checked out my surroundings. No one popped out from the shadows; no one lingered in the darkness… *It was all in my mind.* I took a deep breath and left the safety of my hiding spot to follow the light streaming in from the commotion of the party.

I made it two steps before two rough hands slammed into my back. My arms shot out in enough time to brace myself, keeping my face from hitting the wall. And a strong body pinned me tight against the high-gloss interior, while the grip on my neck kept me locked in place.

"Did you think I didn't recognize you?" he whispered in my ear.

My entire body recoiled as if he'd physically struck me. And the stench of booze filled my nostrils—like he'd bathed in it instead of drinking it. "The very first time I saw you in that little maid getup, I knew it was you. With your breasts pushed up, the sway of that ass, and the pout from those delicious lips. I'd never forget something so sweet. Did you miss me?" His fiery tone burned to the depths of my soul.

My brain faltered as fear rattled me to my core. *It was him—their ringleader.* The masked man with those cold, dead *brown* eyes. So many scenarios, each planned to the most minute detail should our paths cross again, seemed to have escaped my mind as I shook in place. He was going to take me back to hell, and I had absolutely no fight left for the demons awaiting me.

"I know you remember. I know that vault of yours has held on to me all these years. It's almost time for our… *reunion.* Do you feel what you do to me?" He ground his erection into my ass.

"Where is she? I swear to God if she ran again, you're both fucking dead." Dom thundered from the other side of the door.

"Soon, Persephone, soon," the man who haunted my every waking hour whispered as he released my neck. I pushed from the wall, wanting to get a good look at him, to confirm his identity. "Not so fast," he warned and punched me in my side, effectively knocking the wind out of me. I dropped to the ground like a ton of bricks, forced to watch a pair of shiny black shoes as they calmly walked away.

"What the fuck?" Dom yelled, dropping to his haunches in front of me. "Who the fuck put their hands on you?" He helped me to my feet, ordering his goons around with a slew of Italian expletives.

"I don't know. He went. That way." I managed to gasp the words, and his men took off down the hall. "I'm fine. Need to get back out there," I huffed, my mind searching for a clock while realizing I had probably missed my check-in with Carmine.

"Enough of this shit, Perse."

I brushed off his concern and kissed his cheek, adjusting my clothes while beelining for the door. I kept my chin down and weaved through the sides of the party, headed towards the front entrance. I needed to get the message to Carmine before he stormed the venue with hundreds of men and opened fire. Guests were circling Lucky, congratulating him and ass-kissing the future *King of New York.*

My steps faltered, noticing Apollo and an equally large man blocking my path, Bella among them. She was having a panic attack —likely from all the attention she was suddenly garnering.

That was what happened when you were sheltered for so long: you can't handle the pressure. And you certainly can't function when faced with the horrors of the real world. Princesses were meant to stay in their towers. *Too bad, so sad.* I rolled my eyes as she hid behind the man without a name as Apollo spoke into her ear.

Spying on members of the mafia was how you ended up swimming with cement shoes, and I just so happened to need a new pair. So, I stepped closer and listened intently.

Apollo was reminding the bride-to-be of her station, while she was *in fact* doubting her ability to fulfil it.

Oh, honey, you aren't the only one… This city was fucking doomed if she was their future queen.

I wandered the room for another minute, attempting to find a way to contact Carmine. To no avail. Instead, I was given a front row seat to *dinner and a show* as Gio Moretti accosted his baby sister. Not that I didn't enjoy the sight of his hand marring Bella's perfectly unblemished skin, but the sound as it echoed throughout the ballroom was harsh, even for my liking.

That being said, she had earned just a tad more of my respect when she finally decided to stand up for herself and throw the son of a bitch out—*after* threatening his life. Perhaps she had more balls than I first thought…

I watched Gio's retreating form as he was escorted outside. Though he appeared beaten down—both mentally and physically— he still bore that sadistic gleam. That twinkle that suggested there was more behind the man than his sloppy exterior. His twisted glare locked on to mine, and my entire body seized. His mouth contorted into a cruel smile as he stared at me. Those eyes. That bone structure. His lips parted, and he mouthed a singular word. "Soon."

I was certain that's what he had said anyway—as certain as I could be, knowing my mind liked to play tricks on me. Then, without further preamble, he sent me a wink that trickled fear down my spine and forced me to stumble back a few steps. I plowed into the wall as amusement flashed in his eyes. I grabbed my chest and pressed down over my heart, trying to keep the organ from fleeing its confines.

"I was wrong. Oh, God, was I wrong," I mumbled to myself as the door closed behind him.

As if only really seeing me tonight for the first time, Apollo slowed his steps, his eyes narrowed. I watched his internal conflict while my own raged in both my head and my heart. He wanted to approach me—the tick of his jaw told me as much. But I didn't give him the chance. I turned on my heel and disappeared into the crowd, needing Dom's safety. My mind whirled with the realization that I had fucked up, and I had no idea how to fix it. My thoughts were clouded, and I couldn't get a grip on my teetering sanity. Panic replaced rationality as I searched for Dom or even Carmine. I needed someone to get me out of here before it was too late.

I felt *him*—he was close. But not close enough. I collapsed against the first thing I could grab and tried to gulp in deep breaths, but nothing was helping. Dom and I made eye contact. Then, shoving away from his father, he stormed towards me. I opened my mouth, but nothing came out as my brain, as every neuron, shut itself down—favoring preservation. I needed to talk to him. I needed to explain what happened. I needed to tell him I was sorry for accusing him of being involved. I needed to tell him it wasn't his father. Yes, I was chasing a man who considered himself superior, who profited off the weak while seeking to amass an empire. But that man wasn't Anthony Moretti.

It was his son. It was Gio…

Dom's lips were moving, but I couldn't make out the words, my legs weakening with each step. He acted quickly, tucking his arm under my knees, as his men surrounded us. He darted towards the car, and just as we were about to pull away, I looked through the window. Carmine had his phone to his ear, staring back at me through the glass. I smiled with a nod, silently telling him I was okay. *Even though I really fucking wasn't.*

And then—as it so often did—the world went black.

Chapter Thirteen
PERSEPHONE

My body was jostled from side to side. Groaning in pain, I rolled over and took in my surroundings. A car. I was in a car. Rubbing the heel of my palm into my eye, I pushed from the seat and rested on my knees against the floor. My mind was fatigued and trying to play catch up. I passed out on the car ride home. I remember bits and pieces of Dom trying to calm me, before the doctor gave me a sedative and tucked me into bed. But this wasn't my room…

My heart pounded as the voice greeted me. "Hello, Persephone."

"You." I stared into the brown eyes that had haunted me for years.

He was supposed to be the temperamental, unhinged, jackass brother. He was mocked by Dom and his father, while the Agostinos didn't respect him and wanted to end his miserable existence. The man before me now wasn't who I had seen traipsing around the mafia circles. This was someone new—though not really new, I suppose—since this someone had been hidden just beneath the surface the entire time.

"I don't understand," I muttered.

"Come on, Persephone. You've already let me down once; don't make it a habit." His phone rang and he answered it quickly, discussing a drop location for later in the day.

"You've played everyone." It wasn't a question. "All these years… I had been hunting *you*. You took everything from me!" I unleashed the torment that had been bubbling in the back of my throat as I screeched the words in his direction.

He smirked. Like it was funny. Like my pain amused him—it probably did. "I don't take women without doing my research; it's why I am untouchable." Gio pulled me onto the seat, quickly tying my wrists and ankles. I was fatigued but I still tried—a mere gnat buzzing in his vicinity.

"Why… why me then?" It was disconcerting that I wanted to hear a reason. I wanted to hear why *I* was picked. Why *my* life was ruined. Why he chose me when no one gave me a second look prior to this hell.

"You mean besides the fact that no one would miss you?" I cringed, hating how much his truth hurt. "You're fucking crazy, but it's your intelligence I wanted more. For years, my father has forced us to live under the Agostinos' thumb. He was hot-headed and uncontrolled, and well, you know all of this already, don't you?"

"He killed Sal Junior." There was no use playing dumb. "Mario Agostino knows and held this over his head."

"Yeah. He handed my fucking sister off to the fucking devil and paid them handsomely for fucking decades. He expected *me* to bow down just because he didn't have the balls to do what needed to be done. So, I made my own empire. I became the threat no one would see coming. And now… now I want to take over the city." He cracked his knuckles, leaning back in his seat. "As to where you come in with all this?" He glanced down at me, his eyes evoking a shiver along my spine. "Back then, I was looking to groom someone to be a queen, reigning at my side. You had the attitude, the beauty, and more importantly, the smarts. I know you have a photographic memory, that you store years of images and information inside that pretty little head. You want revenge, right? To hurt everyone who's hurt you?"

"I returned to New York following the container owned by a dummy corp. In 1996, one little piece of paper had your father's name on it."

"Genius, huh? I had the container tied to my old man, filled it with stolen girls, and dumped it on Agostino territory. It was seamless… until you."

When I'd gotten the information on the shipment, I called John. He was a young cop at the time and had investigated my first disappearance from foster care, one of the good ones. When I escaped from the hooded man—no, Gio… When I escaped from *Gio*, I called him with the location, and he took down everyone who survived my wrath.

I opened my vault and let the contents spill, brokering deals to destroy organizations like the one that plagued my soul. John's partnership earned him a career with the FBI. Then, after I got wind of the container coming to New York, I set Dom up to intervene. He thought he was buying guns, but it was filled to the brim with young, innocent girls.

I needed access to both families. Carmine's assumptions were accurate when it came to his adversaries, so it made sense for me to start in the city. With my talent on the pole, Dom was the easiest target, considering he owned one of the hottest strip clubs on the coast. It was just never meant to go where it had with him.

My heart was never supposed to get involved.

When Dom went to get his *merchandise*, he found me inside the container instead. It was our second "chance" meeting, face-to-face anyway, following my audition and the short bout under his employment. I'd been trying to work him over since that night he saved me and—in the same breath—threw me out. I knew there was *something* he could give me. One look inside that container, and his resolve had crumbled while our story was cemented into history.

In order to avoid a jail sentence for attempting to purchase illegal firearms, Dom accepted a deal, becoming the east coast's *most-notorious* flesh supplier—a cover in order to fry the bigger fish. And so, each of us was a willing chess piece in a longer-played game.

Despite how our relationship came to be, Dom tried protecting me as I forced myself to finish my mission. I just had to make sure I returned the favor and protected him.

From his family. From the Agostinos. From the Ragettis.

I think the biggest unforeseeable revelation in all this subterfuge was that, out of everyone we suspected, Gio never made the list. Not once. There were moments I'd second-guessed Dom— moments where I second-guessed myself and my closeness to him— but, no, it was his damn brother.

Speaking of, I hadn't even realized the fucker was still talking until his voice finally broke me from my trance. "Sadly, the position is no longer available, and I can't have you ruining my plans." He turned the car down a broken gravel road. "So, I need your help for something else." He killed the engine and climbed out, walking around to my door.

"Get the fuck off me!" I yelled, trying to fight against his grip on my arm but stumbling with my restrained limbs. "Where are we? What're you doing, Gio?"

My pupils dilated as I took in the scene in front of me: a house, with at least two dozen men scattered along the front porch, all leering at me. I tried dropping myself to the ground, the heaviness of doom weighing me down and freezing my limbs, but Gio yank me forward. I cried—*begged*—knowing it was useless, but not yet accepting my fate.

"Here." My tormentor stopped in front of the group as one man stepped forward. *Alexander Bucharov, the son of Gio's now-dead Russian gun supplier*—information I'd acquired during my time in New York and locked up for safe keeping.

Alexander muttered something in his native tongue, and his *comrades* started laughing. Then he strutted closer, before his hand shot out and groped my breast. He kneaded and crushed the sensitive flesh in a display of cruel amusement as he shoved me to my knees; my tears were his aphrodisiac.

"Shut up, *suka*." He slapped me across the face.

"Where is Bella?" Gio asked.

Motherfucker. I was never going to be good enough. Dom went out of his way to protect his sister. And now, Gio was trading me to the Russians in exchange for her safety. I was looking literal death in the face, and all I could think about was the women I wouldn't be able to save. And yet, the Morettis and the Agostinos only protected their own families. Their own kind. *Fucking selfish bastards.*

"Now? Now you're suddenly worried about your little sister?" I spat at his feet, falling onto my shoulder.

"She was always meant to be a means to an end—to get what I wanted. But Lucky doesn't deserve her." His voice was resolute in the fact, as if he was doing her a favor.

"And I deserve this?" I rolled to my back and stared at the men surrounding me.

"You, for Bella. Two problems, one abduction." He watched the Russians with suspicion.

I had no idea why I bothered, but curiosity got the best of me. "Who replaced me as your queen?" I asked Gio, spitting blood on the ground.

"Sienna Agostino." He crossed his arms over his chest, seemingly pleased with himself. "*Now*, where is my sister?" Gio had been standing there one minute; and then, the next, guns were cocked and he was forcibly removed from the property. Alexander dragged me inside, muttering filthy promises of pain and retribution—for what, I had no fucking clue. He cut my binds free when we entered the house and I acted scared, curling myself into a ball on the ground.

The moment he looked away, I struck, kicking out and knocking him to the floor. I rolled over and latched my arm around his neck, twisting my legs to keep him in place while choking him out. He was too fucking strong, but I had to try.

Within minutes, he'd subdued me and shoved my face into the wall. Two men rushed in and held me in place, as Alexander ripped a cord from a nearby lamp. He wielded it like a whip, shredding the scarred flesh of my back and reopening both physical and mental wounds.

"Put her in the closet. I have a call to make. Lock both the bitches together," Alexander ordered, his men dragging my battered body from the room.

"No! No!" I begged, as soon as my makeshift prison was in eyesight. But my fight was futile, my pleas falling on apathetic ears. The men shoved me into the cramped space, allowing the darkness to take over and destroy my reality.

One of the cruelest torture devices was solitude. Solitude and the absence of light. The dulling of the senses that allowed our brain to properly process our surroundings. Someone could break you by merely forgetting about you. You'd spend minutes, hours, or days—all unbeknownst to you—questioning when or if they would return.

I was back to the beginning. Back to when my mind and body were first broken. Imprisoned by these men *and* my own fears. I could deal with the pain; the physical abuse told me I was still alive. It was the darkness I couldn't take. Before I was the woman I'd become, I was just a girl locked in a cement cell, deprived of daylight—of any light—and tethered by my own crumbling mental state. And now, I was that girl again.

This… *this* I couldn't handle. This was a darkened cage where terrible monsters would spread lies inside my head, forcing me to question what was and wasn't real. It would snap my reality in half, leaving just the outer shell—a mass of animated flesh and bones, void of conscious thinking. When things got to be too much, I'd found solace in the protection *my room* at Dom's allotted me. He called it *my cage*; he acted like it was a punishment for my misdeeds.

It was neither of those things.

The door was secured with a heavy lock, and the windows were bolted shut—on my side of the room. I controlled who entered *and* when. It was my sanctuary. A safe place, allowing me to escape the world, when outside forces threatened my sanity. And Dom understood my inherent need for stability, *locking* my *cage* as if he could sense me slipping before the last thread of rationality unraveled.

But Dom wasn't here… And I wasn't safe.

Bella was brought in sometime later, begging for them to stop touching her. *Touching her.* She had no clue how easy she was going to have it. Her life would be hell, that much was sure, but not in comparison to my own. She pleaded for Lucky to save her, promising me that her future husband would save me too.

I had no idea why I lied to her about the men raping me, but I did. Her obvious distress at the mere mention of what happened to women like me, women who didn't have a tower to hide away in, made me smile. It offered a brief moment of reprieve. Of the pleasure I took in her anguish. It heightened her fear. I could smell it, taste it, as it slipped through the cracks of the door and satiated an irrational jealousy for the girl who had everything. She didn't deserve my cruelty; she'd been nothing but kind to me. I knew it, but it didn't change a thing. It didn't alleviate the knowledge that they *would* come…

For her. Not me.

Chapter Fourteen
PERSEPHONE

Time ticked by as I felt everything leaving me. I didn't know what was real, which voices were external and which were the echoes of a plagued mind trying to preserve itself. I didn't know if the memory of Apollo carrying me out of that house and taking me back to the Agostino compound was tangible, or if it was all a daydream concocted by the remnants of *that* girl still locked in *that* closet. And worst of all, I didn't know if I'd ever escape *myself*.

Days and weeks moved rapidly, as though I was suspended in time, while Apollo and the Agostinos tried to extort information from a brain that had nothing left to give. The problem was: they were asking all the wrong questions.

"You want to go back that badly?" Apollo asked, helping the doctor hold me down.

I'd been escorted from the Agostino's compound to Apollo's cabin in the mountains, but I refused to make it easy on him. I was tired of being locked up. He'd tried to leave me behind, and I snapped, ramming my head into the door.

"Don't ask questions you already know the answers to." The pounding in my temples created a wave of nausea, my stomach contents churning and threatening to break the surface.

"Back to your cage," he growled, the words dripping with anger.

"What do you know of cages?" I countered, but the blankness that dropped over his eyes told me he was all too familiar with them. "A physical or mental cage? Which one could it be?"

"What the fuck are you talking about?" He was losing his patience, and I couldn't help but smile.

"Tsk, Tsk, Tsk. You of all people, with your… proclivities… You should know the difference. Did my master physically confine me? Lock me up like a beast in a cage? Or did he merely contain what was already spilling over without him, by offering an alternative? As one would toss a bucket under a cracked pipe; whether he was there or not, the water would drip. Drip. Drip. But limiting the area affected by the overflow makes for an easier clean-up." He contemplated my analogy for a moment. "Do I look like the type who'd allow her master to cage her… ever again? No, I don't. So do not judge what you fail to comprehend."

"He cages your emotional outbursts. It's metaphorical?"

I didn't give a fuck that it confused him; he didn't need to understand. I closed my eyes and ignored him until he finally left the room.

I hadn't the slightest clue how long it had been since Apollo had rescued me from the Russians. I'd heard the comments and felt the tension at the cabin, even before they put me in the car bound for the Agostino compound once again. Something was up, and I had a feeling I knew who was on the rise.

The car slowed its approach into the city, my two guards staring at a chaotic scene involving an overturned vehicle and crushed metal—there were no other bystanders in sight of the damage.

"Fucking tourists." The one guard pointed towards the bits of glass on the side of the road.

"Behave yourself, little psycho. Let's see if they need help," the other grunted.

I sat up in the seat, looking out the window, and I couldn't help my sneer as we eased to a stop. Matteo Ragetti stood beside the upturned car, his arms folded across his large chest. He was covered in ink and tall like his brother—though the younger sibling's blank expression seemed a little less daunting. But as I watched him positioned on the side of the road, appearing out of place in his jeans and baseball cap, I chuckled.

"Need some help?" one guard asked, as Matteo approached our passenger side.

"Nah, we don't need help." The California native sighed.

"But you do." Carmine's voice came from our driver's open window, before either guard had time to react. Within seconds, both would-be Good Samaritans had been removed from our SUV, and the Ragetti brothers and I were driving forward. "You all right?"

"I am now." I smiled, breathing deeply for the first time in what felt like years. "You have to get me to the Agostino compound and I need your phone."

Matteo handed me his cell as I made a few calls, arranging to finally put an end to it all. Then I leaned over the seat and told the brothers everything I had confirmed for them: Anthony Moretti. Mario Agostino. Gio Moretti. They were all guilty when it came to creating our pain and suffering over the years. Anthony was a dead man regardless, but Carmine had a personal grievance against Mario for covering it up.

"He's fucking dead," Matteo grunted.

"He deserves worse than that," Carmine added. "And I know exactly how to ensure he gets it." His smile, as it reflected in the rearview mirror, sent chills down my spine.

"Don't make me regret helping you." A bad feeling settled in my gut. "Carmine, I mean it." The car swerved, before pulling up to the curb a block away from the Agostino family home.

Carmine turned in his seat to look at me. "Let me make something fucking clear, so even that pretty little head of yours can understand. You didn't fucking help us; we helped you. We got *you* to the people who gave you your answers. Not the other way around," Carmine snapped, while Matteo's thick arm blocked the irate Italian from leaning into the back seat.

"That's right. You planned to start a fucking war on a whim, without giving a damn about the collateral damage." I crossed my arms over my chest. "Now, you have the proof you need to demand retribution and force Mario to step down."

"Correction: I have the facts *you* wanted cross-referenced before I watched them collapse in on themselves." He threw the car into gear and pulled onto the long driveway of the opulent estate. "Now get the fuck out," he ordered when we idled in front of the house.

Matteo exited the passenger side and opened my door. "John is twenty minutes out. I will wait on the street and ride up with them." He nodded at me, turning back towards the car. "Be careful, Seph. Once the truth is revealed, you'll be a target."

I held my hands over my heart and gave him a sad smile. A minute later, an Agostino goon came outside and locked me back in Apollo's room. I smirked as I took note of the holes I'd made in the walls. He'd picked up the shredded bedding and organized his shelves, but the other damage remained. I grabbed a marker from his desk and wandered towards the bed, still grinning to myself as I left him a message.

"Persephone!" A male voice shouted, as I clicked the marker cap closed, the door flinging open and slamming against the drywall. I followed his call outside the room, feeling free and giddy, my old self stepping out from the terrifying shadows.

The FBI had the Agostino house surrounded, all the male occupants now lying on their stomachs with their hands cuffed behind their backs. Bella stood with her parents near the door, their hands raised in the air in surrender. I couldn't hold back my gloating as I skipped over each of the prone figures, especially as Apollo's large body turned sideways to see me passing. Dom emerged from one of the blacked-out vans, opening his arms, and I jumped into his warm embrace.

"You missed me," I stated, making him chuckle.

"Maybe a little." He kissed the tip of my nose. "You're a fucking mess."

"But I'm *your* fucking mess," I taunted, as we stood near an idling car with John.

"Let me get changed, and I will come with you. I want to see his face. *I need to see it.*" I smiled at John, my lips dropping when he responded by grabbing my arm and tugging me behind him.

No…

"Dominic Moretti, you're under arrest." John stepped forward.

If looks could kill, Dom's glare was like a 9mm to my temple.

Pure loathing rippled off him in waves as I scrambled to fully grasp the situation. I had nothing to do with this… I was just as confused as he was.

"What? John, don't joke." *Because it wasn't funny.* But he ignored my pleas as his cuffs dropped down and latched in place around Dom's wrists.

"Quite the plot twist: the honeypot appears to have fucked us both." Even face-down in the dirt and gravel, Apollo had a way of appearing self-assured as he stared at Dom in challenge. "I do mean *literally* and metaphorically, of course."

It took a moment for the words to sink in, but when they did, Dom lashed out like a rabid dog tugging on his leash. "You mother-fucker!" He shook John loose, stepping over bodies to land his boot against Apollo's grinning face—the resounding crack of flesh and bone both terrifying and deafening. "I've heard you're into some fucked-up shit, but I didn't think rape was one of them. You fucking took advantage of her, you son of a bitch!"

"Did I?" Apollo laughed, spitting blood onto the concrete. "Or did she beg me for it?"

"I'll fucking kill you. You were supposed to protect her!" Dom was still cuffed and fighting against John as the FBI agent attempted to pull him back for a second time. "You damn well knew she was fucked up! She barely knew who the fuck she was!"

"Then what's your excuse?" Apollo countered, earning himself one more kick to his side before John finally gained the upper hand.

"She's mine!" Even as he stared at me with pure disgust, hearing his declaration of ownership made me… happy.

After uncovering what I'd done, *everything* I'd done, Dom was still defending me. I *had* been lost, and in a place where I could've been manipulated into my actions… but I was unsure if that had really been the case with Apollo. I'd been in control during the exchange. I'd forced him to bend to my whims. And I'd taken what I knew belonged to someone else. To Sienna Agostino—at least in her mind. And it felt good to one-up the bratty rich girl. Sexual favors were a currency in my world. It was what I had been taught, how I survived and self-soothed. So, the morality behind it all was gray, to say the least. And who was using whom was subjective. But sex and emotions were two vastly different categories, and my heart belonged to Dominic Moretti long before I even acknowledged it.

"What're the charges?" Dom asked, scowling in my direction.

"Murder," John responded, before shoving him into a black SUV while ordering me to stay back.

Gabriel. I'd witnessed Dom beat the fucker to death for assaulting me. And *I* was the reason he was getting arrested, but John was supposed to save us. *Both of us.*

"We had a deal!" I screamed, fighting my way towards the vehicle. "I've given you years of my time, years of information to help your career, and we made a *fucking* deal, John!"

"But you failed to include Dominic Moretti in that deal, Persephone. And why the fuck do you care what happens to him anyway? This is over; you're going back to California." John threw me under the bus and didn't even flinch as the wheels ground me into the figurative pavement. "The Ragettis are waiting for you."

"You fucking bitch." Dom spit in my face and lunged forward, causing John to stumble. "The Ragettis, Persephone? You conniving little whore!"

Apparently, that was where he drew the line…

"It's not what you think, Dom! Please!" My limbs locked in place as my heart shattered into a million pieces.

"Get me the fuck out of here before you have to pin *two* murders on me." Dom shrugged free of John's hold, climbing into the SUV on his own accord.

"Don't look at me like that, Perse. You knew this was coming all along." John stared me down with cold indifference.

Dom glared at me through the window. "You're fucking dead to me." He spit the words like they were venom, leaning back in his seat as the vehicle pulled away, and John escorted me to the van headed towards Dom's mansion.

"The end was always meant to be Gio's ruin—even if I didn't know it was *him* at the time. Never Dom's." I felt a traitorous tear drip down my cheek. "I… I don't want to go back. My deal with

Cali is done," I muttered pitifully as we came to a stop, and a car pulled up behind the van.

Matteo walked over to my side. "It's circumstantial at best. His attorney will have him out in two weeks… tops." He stared down at me, unmoved by my tears. "Want to grab your stuff?"

I turned towards the house that I thought of as my home, as my safe place, and sharp pokers stabbed at my chest. "Nothing belongs to me." I pivoted on my heel without another word and climbed into the car, closing the door on all the pain and misery my own decisions had inevitably inflicted.

Chapter Fifteen
PERSEPHONE

My heart was in turmoil; there was no other explanation for the hollowness inside my chest. The *only* person in my entire life who actually helped me—who kept the shadows from descending over my soul and swallowing it whole—was gone. And I had no one to blame but myself.

It didn't matter that my relationship with the Ragettis was strictly platonic; they were the enemy. Dom's father killed Carmine's uncle, and the Ragettis wanted their revenge. He knew it all now… knew I was here, with their help. It was a betrayal; lying by omission.

I didn't tell him I came from California, specifically looking for him. *For his family.* I didn't tell him it was the Ragettis who financed my endeavor. I didn't tell him that no matter how much I craved his touch, yearned for his affection, and fought his hold on me, I also loved him.

That he was the beacon of light in the darkness surrounding me. That every time I felt myself slipping into a new hell I was sure I would never recover from, he'd pull me out like it was nothing.

Instead, I kept my mouth shut, swallowed my emotions, and hyper-focused on my need for revenge. All the while, I was destroying myself. And I had no one to blame but the dumb-blonde-bitch looking back at me in the mirror.

I hated her. I hated what she'd done to us. What *I'd* done. There was only one way to make this right, and I could only hope that it would be enough.

"Ready?" Matteo startled me from my pathetic thoughts. "They have eyes on him and don't want to miss their opening." I nodded and hopped into his car, before we pulled up to an abandoned ware-house a short time later.

During my *second* bout of forced captivity, I'd overheard Gio talking about an upcoming deal and where he planned to meet for the exchange. And after my rescue, I relayed the information to John.

The place was surrounded. I couldn't see them, but I knew the Feds were everywhere. The agents prepared themselves for entry—this was where all my hard work and personal strife would come to fruition, exploding in an epic display of cosmic payback.

We walked over to the covert surveillance van. Peering into the window, I watched the portable monitor. Gio was leaning against the building, his hands in his pockets. His entire demeanor was wrong, completely off-kilter when it came to any of the personalities I'd observed him display.

"Something's not right," I muttered, garnering Matteo's atten-tion. "He knows we're here."

"It's too late." John smiled, calling *go* into his radio.

My focus stayed on Gio as chaos erupted around him. Men fled like cockroaches in the daylight—all but one—as the Feds flew in and corralled them into a circle. Gio didn't move, not a single inch. His smile was knowing and… cocky. *What the fuck was up his sleeve?*

As it all dwindled down, I tried swallowing past the lump in my throat as I approached the agents now detaining my longtime adver-sary. Taking a deep breath, I threw on my *crazy* smirk and held my head high.

"Look who it is," greeted the voice and cold eyes of the man who'd abducted me all those years ago. "I've missed you."

"I've waited for this moment for longer than I care to admit.

Your game is up, Moretti." I smirked, but his expression told me he knew my strength was a farce.

"Did you dream about me? Did you rack your brain for even the most basic memory that would *somehow* point towards *something*? When you went to California and came back, did you see me in every customer you entertained? You may have been hunting me, but I was the one with eyes on you." The intense glare was what I remembered. I shook as I was catapulted back… to when this man owned me: mind, body, and soul. No matter how I struggled against it.

"Giovanni Moretti, you're under arrest…" One of the Feds stepped forward, grabbing Gio by his bicep and dragging him away. But our gazes were glued to one another, his hold over me unbreakable. Even now.

"I'm going to want a phone call, and I need an attorney. But if *you* want something *from* me, *you'll* need to do something *for* me." He commanded me, despite the shackles commanding him.

"What?" I whispered, internally scolding myself for showing weakness.

He leaned forward. "We both know you want more. You want names. And I have them all. I want a visit with Sienna Agostino. Now." And then he was gone. If I gave him this, he'd hand over the other big fish.

"Persephone, breathe," John ordered, and I slowly forced air into my lungs.

"Fuck you, John." I still hated him for taking Dom from me. I hated that the door to my vault was blown wide open, and every memory was sitting on my shoulders.

My head ticked, my spine tingled, and my legs wobbled as I followed John back to the SUV. *Dom. I needed Dom.* He was my person, the one who made the nightmares go away.

I'd been left to run free, without the security of my master and his leash. Sure, I had teeth and didn't mind baring them when I needed to. But there was no one to protect me from the worst threat out there in that big, bad world: *myself.* Instead, the only man able to lure me home and into the sanctity of my cage was locked in one of his own. With a high probability that the key would be thrown away for life.

And then it clicked.

I needed to do something for him. For us. And most importantly, for myself. Dom wasn't a good guy, not in the slightest. But he was good to me and *for* me. I could feel my sanity slipping in his absence, and it was a daily struggle to maintain it. My mind needed a reprieve, time to heal. "John, I need you to get in touch with Em." He stared at me in shock. "Yes, from Umbra."

Em was someone very similar to me. She came from the same background, but rather than a solo act, she'd amassed an army. An army of men and women, with various talents, all of which she used to aid in her mission. She led an underground movement to destroy those seeking to hurt the innocent—like a more lethal version of Robin Hood. We needed her help. *I* needed her help.

Mental illness wasn't something to joke about. The general public mocked it as if those who bore the burden were weak, seeking attention, or downright faking it. The social pressures and stigma left many of us to suffer in silence, afraid to leave the familiarity of our own personal hells to ask for help. Well, my time in the darkness was over. I would step into the light and fight for my own betterment.

I would make this right. But first, I had to save Dom before I could save myself.

Chapter Sixteen
DOMINIC

I'd been going out of my mind for days. The moment I realized she was gone, it felt like a piece of my sanity had shattered. There was an ache in my chest that now burned like wildfire with the knowledge of her betrayal. I wanted to give that girl *everything*. And all I asked for in return… was her.

She consumed my thoughts and incited my most primal urges—a mystery that had me looking to destroy her before piecing the remnants back together again. She was my favorite puzzle: intricate, complex, and challenging. Everything a man needed to keep him from straying, to captivate his attention.

We were toxic, and that was exciting. Addicting. Until that son of a bitch got between us.

John Hardwicke was dirty, a disgusting FBI *stronzo*. We'd crossed paths when he was hunting down members of the cartel. And we'd worked out a deal: he scratched my back and I scratched his, under the radar of course. I didn't know he was FBI, at first, not until the incident at the docks with my *misappropriated* gun supply.

John had reached out that night, giving me a heads up about a shipment scheduled to land. He would seize the bulk of it, and I could take a portion. *At cost.* What neither of us expected—which

I now realize was a setup—was the contents of that container being a little less semi-automatic and assault, and a little more flesh and bone. No guns, just women. And Persephone was locked inside.

She'd drilled her way through my chest and into my heart. *She needed me.* And only I could protect her.

But this entire fucking time she had been working with the enemy—the fucking Ragettis. *The FBI.* And at this point, I didn't know which blow stung worse.

I had absolutely no idea what I was going to do about it. Or her. She was already so broken, a shell of a human being, after the shit hand she'd been dealt in life. Which was exactly why her... *interaction* with the Agostino guard dog—while distasteful—said more about him and his integrity, than it did about her and her overall loyalty to me.

But this... *this* I couldn't forgive.

I'd happily rot in this fucking jail cell for what I'd done. I didn't regret it or my actions. Yup, I could do my time and sit pretty, knowing she was out there... free of the horrors that plagued her. Of me, and my family name. But not with my fucking enemy. Not with the fucking Ragettis. The more I stared at these walls, the more the knife twisted in my back.

"For as damaged as she is, she's fucking fierce when it comes to getting what she wants." John stopped in front of my cell door. "Your lawyer is here for a meeting."

He motioned for another guard to escort me. I turned around, allowing them to cuff my hands behind my back. We moved slowly down the narrow hallway, other inmates leaning against the bars to get a look at the action.

"Your brother is also here." John chuckled when my neck snapped in his direction. "Persephone closed out her deal with us. We secured the head of the trafficking syndicate, and we granted her one wish."

We started moving forward again, my mind filled with the chaos that was my reality. My brother, the *fottuto idiota*, was captured. The goddamn international kingpin of flesh trafficking. *My brother.* The

Moretti son everyone believed was no more than a hot-headed moron. Well, he fucking surprised us all.

"It was borderline anticlimactic honestly. For all the blood, sweat, and tears she shed, the takedown was uneventful. Almost like he *wanted* to be caught," John admitted, opening a door and leading me towards the interrogation rooms.

The whine of the door opening on its hinges had us pausing mid-stride, before the cascade of long blonde hair and sex-in-a-pencil-skirt stepped into the hallway. Even after she handed me over to the Feds on a fucking platter, my heart ached for her. I was the one who calmed her nightmares and kept her head on straight. The one who picked her up off the ground after each mission ended and more girls were saved. I gave her life, and here she was, handing me death.

"Dom." It came out as a whisper.

But I couldn't speak to her, because I knew I would break. So, instead, I glared at the woman with one hand still clawing through my rib cage, enjoying how she flinched as the flames of hatred flickered across her skin.

I glanced past her and saw Gio handcuffed to a table, Sienna Agostino sitting across from him. He was staring at the woman like she was his next meal, his mask of idiocy dropped now that his true nature was known. He glanced in my direction for a single moment, his eyes dancing between Persephone and me and his lips lifting in amusement. He knew she'd taken us both down—two mafia legacies bested by this slip of a girl.

"Dom." Persephone tried again, but I kept my back to her. "John. We had a fucking deal."

"We did, Perse. I will keep up my end, like I promised. But a few more days in jail won't hurt him." The bastard chuckled, practically shoving me through the doorway and towards my lawyer.

"What the fuck is going on?" I asked the chubby man in a suit, now sweating under my glare.

"You're being released. A deal was struck and they're dragging their feet, but you're a free man," he explained.

"What deal?" I growled, agitated he didn't consult with me.

"Someone else confessed to the murder." *Motherfucker*. I knew exactly who that *someone* was, without even having to be told. "They confessed, and in exchange, you're being released—all charges dropped."

My neck twisted towards the glass partition in the door. Persephone was standing there, watching me with tears in her eyes. *She wouldn't*. No. Fucking. Way. I rose to my feet, tugging on the shackles tethering me to the table. My lawyer's argumentative tone disappeared into the background as I stared at her.

I love you. She mouthed the words to me, before a figure appeared behind her. Matteo-fucking-Ragetti.

"She has an excellent case, if she pleads insanity." The fat fucker in front of me was still speaking, as the blonde enigma turned and disappeared around a corner.

"Get her the fuck out of it," I growled at him, as armed guards entered the room to drag me back to my cell. "Get me the fuck out of here, then get her ass out of it!" I shouted from the hall.

This couldn't happen. I wouldn't allow it. As much as I hated her for all the deception, for aligning herself with the Ragettis, the girl didn't deserve to go to jail for something she didn't do. For something *I* did. She'd already spent most of her life under lock and key, suffering for the sins of others. I wouldn't let it continue.

"She wants to get help," John said the moment I was shoved back behind the bars of my steel cage. "It's her apology for the lies. But also, she wants the help being institutionalized has to offer. It's her only chance of survival, now that her mission is complete."

"That shows how much you really don't know her. Her mission will never be *complete*. When one monster is put down, another jumps in his spot," I muttered, sitting on the hard bench.

"She needs to heal, and then *someone* needs to stop her. It *will* kill her, if she keeps it up. We've eradicated hundreds of trafficking rings because of her; she deserves to make peace within herself."

"How did she do so much for you, and yet you're allowing her to confess to a crime she didn't commit?" I was appalled by his callousness—she'd handed this man his career, his shiny badge, and his lucrative paycheck.

"I kept up my end of the deal. It's not my fault she didn't think to amend hers." His smirk dropped with my next words.

"That's bullshit and you know it," I hissed, and his face paled. "You're fucking pathetic. A coward. I thought you cared about her."

"I do. That's why you're going free, and I'm granting her the concession." When I glowered at him, he continued, "She wants to heal herself, to do it on her own. I can't make it any clearer for you." And then he walked off.

They took their sweet time organizing my release, but the confines of that cell gave me an opportunity to think. She'd betrayed me. She'd lied, manipulated, and destroyed a large part of me in the process. I should walk away from her—forever.

On the other hand, she *was* gorgeous. And a great fuck. Persephone tugged at my heartstrings, even from a distance. *She loved me.* In her own fucked-up way. And I loved her… in mine.

So, after everything, it wasn't really a choice. I'd be there to protect her, to get her ass out of the mess we'd both created. Then I would spank that same fucking ass—over and over—before driving into it. All, just to make a fucking point: *I was in charge.*

And soon, she'd realize it too.

Epilogue
PERSEPHONE

"*You have been found not guilty by reason of insanity or mental defect. This court hereby sentences you to the Manhattan Psychiatric Center, until such time as a treating physician deems you fit to be released back into society,*" the judge announced, before hammering the gavel.

I wasn't an idiot. I knew the court-mandated hospital was no coincidence, and had everything to do with Dom's coercion. I was a nobody. I didn't come from money. And I'd *killed* someone. Well, I'd actually killed several *someones*, just not that one in particular. But Dom's imprisonment was a wrong I needed to right.

This. This was also for me. If I was in the real world, outside a clinical setting, I'd continue to allow other people to be my solace. I needed to establish peace within myself. Without *him*. And this was how I'd do it.

Days, weeks, months, years. Who knew? Since most nights felt very much like the last… *The same.* And I lost count. But in time, I started to feel like—what I was told—was *normal*. My normal anyway, considering I still felt like I would crawl out of my skin and was often plagued by boredom. *That*, apparently, was showing I was gaining control and on the right path. I didn't… *hate* it. It would just take some time to get used to the change.

I quickly learned that having a hobby was a good thing, so I started writing. I found it cathartic; it allowed me a momentary escape from my miserable existence, giving me a sense of sanity that was enjoyable. The doctors balanced my mood swings with medication and alternative approaches—things I hadn't tried before—since my usual methods had involved lashing out and sleeping for days.

And just as suddenly as my world had fallen apart, I felt ready to enter society again. I'd been told three times now that I was *cleared* to go. I could only assume that the doctors and their families had been threatened by *someone*. So, I sent a message through John, stating that prolonged treatment had been my decision. That I was staying.

I'd gotten visitation requests… and I denied them. I refused to see *him* until I was ready. John was my only tie to what was happening outside these walls; he'd update me on all the key figures they'd uncovered after Gio's bust. Slowly but surely, they were making progress, dismantling the skin trade from the top down. I focused on that small victory, because I knew I was a major part of it.

"Ready?" John asked, standing at my door.

I took a long look around the room, one last time, before swinging my bag over my shoulder and following him out. Each gate that buzzed and opened, each door I stepped through, offered another measure of peace. I was an entirely new person, and yet I was completely the same.

"All arrangements have been made, but I want you to know you have options." John stopped at the last door, the last lock barring my freedom.

"We both know that won't happen." I smiled. I could *feel* him on the other side, my heart leaping out of my chest to close the distance.

I was nervous.

"I know, but the offer is there if you ever need it." John turned the handle. "I'm glad you're feeling better, Perse."

"Me too," I muttered, wincing as the sunlight assaulted my eyes. I blinked a few times before I was able to focus and see him leaning against the wall. In his trademark suit, arms folded across his even larger chest, and a lazy smirk on his face. He was even more hand-some and daunting than I remembered. I walked towards him on slow, shaky legs—a throng of butterflies erupting in my stomach and my palms sweating.

Before I could open my mouth, his calloused hands grabbed my chin and forced my eyes upwards. His expression was blank, but also hard and unrelenting, as I melted beneath his scrutiny. I gulped—audibly—my breath stuck in my throat as I debated what to say. But just as I was ready to pull back, a seductive smile emerged and soft-ened his chiseled features.

"There she is," he whispered and pulled me in for a kiss.

Yes, here I am.

For the first time in my life, I really was present. I felt content. And whole. My mission would never be done; there would always be someone out there who needed my protection. But it was a euphoric sensation, to finally be able to live in my own skin. To seek justice, rather than focus on revenge. To win the battle, without losing parts of myself.

The moment his lips touched mine, I knew this was it. *I was home.* Dominic Moretti was domineering and demanding. In every facet of his life. He was also bullheaded. Overbearing. *Masochistic…* He could bring out the worst in me at times, but it was always in an effort to salvage the best of me. To protect the fragile parts I'd only just learned to accept. He was the restraint to my lack thereof, while I was an outlet for his inner turmoil. It didn't matter if we made sense, because there was so much beauty in the chaos.

Even though I knew I was more than strong enough on my own, I now had Dom to catch me when I stumbled. *Because I would stumble —we all would.* And it didn't hurt to have someone so *fucking* sexy helping you up. Besides, I was still waiting for the delicious punish-ment his eyes currently promised. After all, I had been a very naughty girl.

Epilogue
DOMINIC

*S*he blocked all my attempts to contact her. She wouldn't allow me to see her and wouldn't answer my calls. Her treating physician had a beautiful wife and two small children—he was also very eager to discharge her upon request.

And my little pet had refused. John tried to block me on all communicative platforms, promising me she was fine while reinforcing her need for autonomy.

That didn't mean I was obliging. I was proud she was seeking the help she deserved, but my palms tingled with the need for physical reprisal. Her punishment wasn't something she could run from forever. That time would come—*eventually*. She would return home with me, and her ass would meet the back end of my hand.

My life had been a whirlwind since she left me. I threw myself into my businesses, and the increased productivity proved very lucrative. I'd needed to stay busy to avoid showing up at the hospital and stealing her—consequences be damned. She'd burrowed herself into my heart, and even though I felt like I was drowning, I'd made a promise to do better by her.

Carmine Ragetti had sent me a message, saying that *it wasn't personal*, which I didn't believe at all. It had always been about my father, who—if we were being honest—got what was coming to him. And now that Pops was dead, the Ragettis had moved on to their next target. Thanks to Persephone, a whole new violent storm had come from the west, looking to brutalize the east.

They'd protected her at a time when I couldn't. I knew she relied on the brothers to keep her going. And because of that, she was the only thing *keeping* them alive—for now.

Gio was locked in prison for a multitude of offenses, but my darling brother was nothing if not a strategist. His story was almost too insane to be plausible.

He tried sending messages to Perse, and thankfully John blocked those as well. She didn't need his voice inside her head anymore, and John ensured she knew nothing of the chaos he was creating outside it either.

My baby sister was happy with her new husband and, more importantly, *protected*. I was going to be an uncle and as much as I hated to be near *that* family, seeing my sister content and blossoming unburdened a part of me that still blamed myself for sending her away. While another part longed for the same thing with my woman. With my pet.

"If you hurt her in any way… Physical… emotional… I don't give a fuck which. Fuck the paperwork, I'll kill you myself," John said at my back as I leaned against the hospital wall.

"I don't doubt that." I didn't turn to look at him, staring at my watch with impatience.

"I can't believe the shitstorm surrounding your brother all this time," he remarked offhandedly.

Gio wasn't cooperating to save his ass. He was doing it because he didn't like being beat. Like a bratty kid tipping the gameboard, my brother was dismantling his empire just because he could.

"I'll go get our girl." John went to walk past me, but I moved quickly: shoving him against the abrasive brick exterior, gripping him by the throat, and pinning him in place with my forearm across his chest.

"She's mine," I growled, pausing a beat before releasing my hold.

"Roger that." He smirked, heading towards the entrance.

"What the fuck?" I muttered this to myself. I was on pins and needles waiting for my girl. It seemed like years before I heard the door click open.

She stepped into the sunlight, and my heart seized in my chest. This woman turned me on, made me murderous, and filled my heart with adulation—all with one glance. She wore loose linen pants and a lazy shirt that revealed her tight stomach. She'd put on a little bit of weight, but it was healthy and fit her natural figure. As I pushed forward and approached her, my pulse pounded in my throat, both in fear and excitement. I wondered what exactly I would see when I looked into her eyes.

I twisted her face towards mine and sighed in relief. The blue eyes of an angel stared back at me, clear and alert. She was no longer plagued by her demons, nor was she shrouded by darkness. The heaviness in her soul had lifted, and gone was the girl who teetered on the edge of insanity and self-injury. I would always be there should she slip, but it was a sight to behold, finally seeing her at peace with herself.

"There she is," I whispered. "Ready to head home?"

"I hear I have a new home." It wasn't a question; I knew John was keeping tabs on me. I wanted us to have a fresh start. So, as I increased my profit flow, I decided that a new start meant a new environment. She didn't need a *cage* anymore. So, I built us a sanctuary instead. Today was the culmination of our cliché. Yes, this was the end to our *fairy tale*.

"But first..." I tugged her against me and smirked at the shivers racking her body. "You've been bad, little pet. And I think you need to be punished."

She pulled back and glanced up at me. A slow, devilish smile took over her features, and I found myself smiling back. "Yes, sir," she crooned.

And, as they say, we lived happily-fucking-ever-after.

THE END

About the Author

About the Author

Corporate sales by day, closet romance novelist at night—Dahlia Reign has always had an unparalleled taste for dreamy alpha-men. In her youth, Dahlia had journals by the stacks that she used to jot down her innermost thoughts; subsequently, turning them into romantic stories. Now, years later and with her picturesque alpha-man at her side, she's taken the literary world by storm. Her man, her pittie and an overactive imagination mixed with her bleeding heart—she's set off to tell the world her stories. Buck up and grab a bandaid, shit's about to get heavy.

Other Titles
Agostino Crime Family Series
Contracted to the Devil
Clever as the Devil
Beautiful Deception
& Twice as Twisted
La Reina de Escorpiones Duet
Infinite Sorrow
Endless Deceit

www.ingramcontent.com/pod-product-compliance
Lightning Source LLC
Chambersburg PA
CBHW060501300726
48975CB00008B/2590